OKLAHOMA SUNSHINE

THE MCINTYRE MEN
BOOK SIX

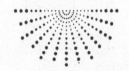

MAGGIE SHAYNE

OLIVERHEBERBOOKS

PUBLISHER'S NOTE: This is a work of fiction. Names, characters, places, and incidents either are the product of the author's imagination or are used fictitiously. Any resemblance to actual persons, living or dead, business establishments, events, or locales is entirely coincidental.

Copyright © 2014 by Maggie Shayne

Published by Oliver-Heber Books

0 9 8 7 6 5 4 3 2 1

❀ Created with Vellum

CHAPTER 1

15 YEARS AGO

*M*ary braced up when she approached her dad. She was as likely to get backhanded as not, so she always braced up when she left her room in whatever house they lived in. Right now it was a doublewide with three whole bedrooms in the woods outside town. Three bedrooms meant she got one of her own. If there were only two, she'd have to sleep on the couch, and she hated sleeping on the couch because it smelled like beer and cigarettes.

Her dad was sitting at the kitchen table. He was drinking a beer, smoking a cigarette, and eating a peanut butter chocolate chip cookie. She'd baked a big batch yesterday, and it had put him in a good mood for all of ten minutes.

Her mom used to bake. She didn't remember, but he'd said so often enough.

That he was eating the cookie was a good sign, but that he was looking at the 'net cancelled it out. The internet always got him going. Maybe this wasn't the best time. Her brother Braxton was with him. Brax was eight and already hated her guts. And he was *always* with their father. She stood still a minute trying to decide.

1

"Spit, it out kid. What do you want now?" her father asked without looking up from his computer.

She took a deep breath, lifted her chin. "I want to play softball."

"*Soft*ball? Psssh. Softball. You getting this Brax? Little Mary Sunlight wants to play softball. What makes you think you'd even make the cut, kid? They have tryouts for that sort of thing, you know. You have to be good.

"Tryouts were today. Coach said I have the makings of a great pitcher. She thinks I could be good."

Her brother made big eyes at her. "*You* made the team?"

"Only two other fifth graders got picked. Everyone else is older."

"I bet the competition was *fierce*," her father said, making it clear he meant the opposite. "Softball. Jeeze, if you play anything, you oughtta pick a real sport."

She did not back down. It was really hard to disagree with her father, and she knew was risking a solid backhand across the face by trying. But this was important to her. "I'll have to stay after school for practice during the season, but there's a late bus so you won't have to pick me up or anything."

"And who the hell's gonna make dinner if you're off playing softball? You ungrateful little shit."

She closed her eyes, cowed and frightened. But this was important. Head low, voice soft, she said, "I'll still have dinner on the table by six, Dad. And on game nights, I'll cook ahead of time so all you'll have to do is heat it up."

"She sure as hell won't have time for desserts," Braxton complained, not to her, to their old man. He barely bothered to acknowledge her as a living being. She was more like a piece of furniture to him.

"I'll do all the baking for the week on weekends," she said. "That's not hard. Anyway, it would save on the gas bill, baking everything at once."

He father narrowed his eyes and looked right at her, instead of through her. "I don't like it. Girls aren't meant to play sports. It'll turn you."

Her brother laughed, and started singing, "Mary's a lesbo, Mary's a lesbo..."

Her cheeks burned. "If I don't play, people are gonna wonder why. Everyone at school saw the tryouts." There was nothing her father hated more than school officials poking around his life. He'd given her a black eye once, and her teacher had asked her over and over what happened. She might've given different answers on different days, though she'd never ratted out her father. Still, social services had shown up at the front door a few days later.

He had never hit her where it would show again. So, she knew he feared that, if he feared anything.

He thought for a long time, then took another bite of the cookie. "The first time you're late or I go hungry, it ends." Then, just to show he wasn't really giving in, he elbowed Brax. "I give it a week, how 'bout you?"

"Three days. She's lazy, and the softball players have to run laps."

They laughed together. Mary turned and went back to her room.

"Aw, I think you hurt her feelings. Your feelings hurt, Little Mary Sunlight? Are they?"

She closed her bedroom door, careful not to slam it. If she slammed it, he'd surge in there like a bull and knock her around to teach her some respect. She hated when he called her Mary Sunlight. Her mother used to call her that. Sometimes, she'd just hold her close and dance around the room, singing "Little Mary Sunlight" to her. It was one of a handful of foggy memories that were all she had of her mom. Becky Beauregard had died a long, long time ago.

Mary took the framed photograph off its crooked nail in the

wall and traced her mother's face. She was so beautiful, hair just like sunshine, and that sunny smile on her face, too. She wore a pretty dress, pale blue, and white beads around her neck, pearls or whatever.

"Why'd you have to die?" she whispered. Tears welled up and rolled down her cheeks.

CHAPTER 2

PRESENT DAY

*J*ason swung the hammer in a steady, soothing cadence. Around and down. Around and down. Every blow shaped the red-hot steel on the anvil more. His body was damp with sweat, both from the heat of the forge and the exertion of swinging that hammer.

The trick was to get in as many blows as possible before the metal began to cool. And there was a knack to knowing just when that was. One swing too many, the blade cracks, and it's over.

But it wouldn't take too many more. This beauty was nearly done. He took the smaller hammer and went up and down the blade, perfecting the shape. And then he heated it once more, gave a final inspection, and doused it in a vat of oil.

The hiss of the steam from the oil and the smell of hot metal were satisfying in a way he could never describe to anyone else, which was why he hadn't bothered to try.

This was *his* thing. He didn't share it.

Using the tongs, he took the blade out, held it at arm's length, tipped it left and right as he eyed its edge. Not a ripple. Not a bend. Perfection. It was ready to be honed, polished. He had a handle ready and waiting; intricately carved bone in the shape of an elk's head, stylized, long and slender, but you could still tell what it was.

He put the blade on the workbench, took off his goggles, his apron, his oversized leather gloves, and shut down the forge. And only when everything in the workshop was where it belonged, did he go back inside and straight through to the shower.

And as always happened when he wasn't working at the forge, his brain kicked into overdrive. He'd been working day and night to avoid thinking about what needed thinking about, but he had to stop sometime. He had to think sometime. He couldn't put this off much longer.

He was going to propose to Sunny Cantrell, the sweetest girl in Oklahoma.

He cranked the knobs, stripped down and stepped into the spray. Then he washed and worried until a voice coming from his living room forced him to call it. Grabbing a towel and wrapping it around him, he opened the door a crack to peer out. His brother Rob stood there grinning at him. Jason gave a quick look at his shop door to be sure it was closed. It was.

"I brought you a beer," Rob said, holding up the bottle.

"That's perfect. I was just wishing for a beer. Gimme a sec?"

Rob nodded, sashaying into the living room to plunk himself on the sofa and twist the cap off his long neck. Wrapped in a towel, Tarzan style, Jason left wet footprints all the way to his bedroom where he pulled on a pair of pants. He scrubbed his hair with the towel on his way back out, tossed it behind him and missed the hamper.

"What brings you here, little bro?"

"My better half, mainly."

Jason went to the easy chair, picking up his beer on the way by. "Kiley sent you?"

"Yeah, with a message."

"For me? You sure it's not for Sunny?" Sunny and Kiley and Angie Wakeland had been hanging out since last summer. All the girls were friendly, but that trio had become really tight.

"No, it's for you. It's *about* Sunny, though."

"Well, by all means, deliver the message." He tipped his bottle Rob's way.

Rob stood up and cleared his throat. "Sunny Cantrell is the prettiest, happiest, most successful female in this town, and I have lost my baby weight now–"

"You have, have you?"

Jason scowled at him. "This is Kiley talking."

"I don't think so. Her voice is higher, and she's easier on the eyes."

"Do you mind if I finish?"

He waved a hand. "I can hardly wait."

"I have lost my baby weight now and will look great in my bridesmaid's gown. So get your ass in gear before some other guy comes along and steals her right out from under your slow-moving nose."

He just sat there a sec. Rob returned to his seat, took his beer off the coffee table and drank a big gulp.

"That's quite the message."

"Yeah." He burped. "The beer was my idea. You're welcome."

"Huh. I gotta say, her timing is interesting. Stay right there." He got up, went into the kitchen, opened a cabinet and took out a box of brownie mix.

"Are we baking, bro?"

"Nah. It's the only place I knew she'd never find it. She wouldn't be caught within ten feet of a mix." He opened the box, tipped it up, and out came the little white box.

Rob jumped to his feet. "Holy Smokes, you're really gonna do it!" He surged to the kitchen and snatched the ring box right out of his hand.

"I really am."

7

Rob opened the box and turned it one way and another to make the diamonds sparkle. "I think Kiley will approve."

Jason took the box back, snapped the lid closed. "Yeah, well, don't tell her. No point in her being disappointed if Sunny says no."

"What the–Sunny isn't gonna say no. Why would she say no? You two have been seeing each other for what, four years now?"

"Almost five." He put the ring back in the brownie box, returned it to the cupboard, top shelf, way back.

"She actually might. I would've popped the question before now, otherwise, but every time I bring up anything about...you know, a future together, she gets all funny."

"Funny how?" Rob asked.

"Funny like she suddenly has to leave, or go to the bathroom, or she spills her sweet tea or something."

"On purpose?"

Jason shrugged.

"So, if you don't think she wants it, then why are you asking?"

He heaved a huge sigh. "Because *I* want it. And if she doesn't, well at least she'll have to say so."

Rob whistled a pretty good impression of a bomb falling as he dropped onto the sofa and said, "I think we're gonna need more beer."

"I just...this feels so stupid. What are we, teenage girls?"

"Yeah, we're teenage girls. Tell me what's going on with you, Jason. I'm your brother, come on."

Jason took a deep breath. "I want what you and Joey have. And I want kids. Every time I hold your little Diana or take Matilda Louise on a piggy back ride, I just about lose it. I want a family and I want it with her."

"And you don't think she wants that, too?"

"That's what I'm about to find out." He went back to the kitchen, picking up his brother's empty on the way.

"When? Today?"

"Tonight, I hope."

"And I can't tell Kiley?"

"No, because she'll tell Sunny—instantly. And you know it."

"Yeah," he said. "I know it. But damn, when I get home, she's gonna want to hear how this all went. You know, what you said when I gave you the message."

"Tell her I said thanks for caring, and I'm taking it under advisement."

The text that popped up on Sunny's cell phone said, "We need to talk. Can I come over tonight?"

Sunny was at the bakery's front counter counting up the day's take and putting the cash into a bank bag. She set the bag down and stared at the phone. Her heart sank a little.

"Everything okay, boss?

She glanced up at Mouse, who'd got his nickname as much for his large ears as for his actual first name, Mickey. He'd just finished mopping the main floor and was pushing his wheeled bucket toward the back. "Everything's fine, Mouse. You go on home, you're done for the day."

"On my way."

"Oh, and take this box of pastries with you for Ida Mae." She set the box up on top of the counter, which was really a chest-high glass display case with shelves inside, and a cash register on top.

"Mmm, cheese danish?"

"Go ahead and snatch one for yourself before you hand 'em over. These are leftovers."

He looked up, one brow bent. "But you always send the left-overs to the Tucker Lake Shelter."

Mickey was a former resident of the Tucker Lake Shelter.

9

That was where she'd met him, back when she used to drive the extra baked goods over there herself. "There's plenty for the shelter, I promise. I saved a dozen extra for Ida Mae, and one for you. Go on."

He looked at the box and smiled. "Miss Ida Mae will offer me first choice from the box when I hand it to her. I think she's nursing a crush on me."

He was forty-something. Ida Mae was seventy-something. But she loved having Mickey there. He mowed her lawns, tended her flowers and did light repairs in exchange for room and board. He'd fixed up the second story of the old detached carriage house, and worked at the bakery for pocket-money. He was as happy as a millionaire.

He gave her a nod and a smile, took the box, and headed back.

"Tell Tabitha she can go, too, if she's still in the kitchen."

"Don't worry about that one. Tabitha leaves at five. Not one minute later."

"Gotta love a girl who knows her worth smack outta high school. G'night, Mouse."

"Night, Miss Sunny."

He pushed the mop bucket through the double doors into the kitchen.

Sunny picked up her phone again, re-read the message, and knew what it meant. Jason was going to break up with her. She'd been expecting it for a while now, and while she hated that it was going to happen, she knew it had to. Jason wanted more, she knew he did. He'd brought it up enough times. But she couldn't. She just couldn't.

She'd tried hard not to let things get too serious between them. But as much as she'd held back, she'd become powerfully attached to him. And she cared about him. And she loved being with him. When he wasn't hinting about their future.

They didn't *have* a future.

She should've told him that from the beginning, but she hadn't, and before she knew it, she'd waited too long. So they'd been doing this dance for five years now—dating, hanging out together, sleeping together, attending all his huge family's events together. And all the while, with him trying to get closer and her trying not to.

He wanted more. He was the most eligible bachelor in the state of Oklahoma. He deserved to have what he wanted.

She looked down at the phone. His text looked back at her, unanswered. *We need to talk.* This was kind of heartbreaking. The two of them were good together. She liked having someone who was kind of hers. And he was a good man. A great man, really.

Best man she'd ever known.

She picked up the phone and typed "Just closing up," sent it and realized she was still avoiding the inevitable. Time to face the music. She couldn't get serious with him, and she couldn't tell him why not, and he deserved more. So she keyed in more. "Meet you in the pavilion down back?" It was, she figured, as good a place to be dumped as any, and a better place than most. It was her favorite spot. She almost decided to take it back, suggest somewhere else instead, but he was already replying. The ellipsis dots blinked a coming attraction.

The bell over the door jangled, but she didn't look up until the text came through. "I'll be there in an hour."

"Ah, hell," she whispered.

"Bad news?" Jack Kellogg, her best friend Kiley's father, came up to the counter, smiling his charming smile, dimples digging deep into his cheeks.

"Of course not." She put the phone down and greeted him with her usual sunny smile.

"I've always wondered if that's short for anything. Sunny."

"Nope." She set the phone down. "What can I do for you, Jack?" She wasn't fond of Jack Kellogg. He reminded her of people and things she'd rather forget. He'd done time. But he was Kiley's father, and had allegedly reformed his con-man ways. Because of that, she tried to be polite to Jack and Kendra, Kiley's twin sister, another reformed criminal. But as far as she was concerned, the two of them were not to be trusted.

"Looks like you're closing up. I don't want to–"

"I got distracted and didn't turn the sign over, but don't give it another thought."

"I promised Diana a cookie," he said. "And if I don't bring one back, I'll lose grandpa points."

Kiley and Rob's little girl. Sunny's heart melted at the mention of her name. Both her best friends had children, and she soaked up every bit of kid-time she could, knowing she'd probably never have a family of her own.

"Halfmoons are her favorite," Sunny said. "Wait here." She started to go, then remembered the bank bag was still sitting on the counter. But there was just no discreet way to pick it up now without being obvious. And she didn't want to hurt his feelings.

She sent Jack a smile and headed back into the kitchen, where the leftovers from the day were ready for delivery to the Tucker Lake Shelter. She put four halfmoon cookies into a pink box with white stripes. Her boxes were just like her awning. Each one bore the logo that was also painted on her front window, a bright yellow sun, with SUNNY'S PLACE spelled out above and below, each letter set within a curvy golden ray.

She didn't go behind the counter, and she made herself *not* look at the bank bag as she met Jack in front of it. "Here you go. One for everybody."

"Including me?"

"Including you."

He smiled and said, "You can check if you want. Your money bag's still there."

"Wh-what do you mean?"

"You went back and left an ex-con with your lettuce, so you wouldn't hurt his feelings. You risked a sack of cash just to be nice. Maybe even trusted me a little. I can't even get that much out of my daughter." He gave a shrug and a smile. "Yet."

He handed her a ten-dollar bill, she waved him off. "I already tallied up for the day. These cookies have been written off. If I charge you, I'll go to tax jail."

He took a deep breath, like he was going to say something, but then lowered his head and turned to go.

"What? What were you going to say?"

He looked over his shoulder. "I uh...I have a past. You know that."

"Everyone knows that. It's a small town." But no one knew about hers. She was living a lie in plain sight, and sooner or later, it was bound to come out. She dreaded that day. Jason flashed in her mind's eye, and her heart broke a little. She'd been fighting not to fall in love with him for years.

Jack turned around to face her again, like he'd changed his mind about leaving. "I uh—I don't like when people from my past start coming around Big Falls. I'm a grandpa now. A very young, very handsome grandpa."

"Modest, too," she said smiling. But it felt odd, this conversation. They knew each other, were even friendly, but they didn't talk. Not like this.

"Is someone from your past in town, Jack?"

"Someone I knew in passing yeah. Not to see me—I doubt he even knows I'm here. But you know, I keep up with a few old friends, so I hear things. He's bad news, this guy."

She wanted to ask why he was telling her this, but thought it would be rude. He seemed to really want to get it out. He wouldn't be the first local to come to her out of the blue, wanting to talk out a problem. People really seemed to think she had it all figured out, didn't they? God, if they only knew.

13

He was quiet. Expectant, so she said, "Do you have any idea what he wants in Big Falls?"

"Maybe." He shrugged and looked at his toes. "It's not good, whatever it is."

"Why don't you tell Chief Jimmy?"

"Yeah, I'm still not real comfortable around the law."

"He's not the law, Jack. He's family."

"I think you're stretching it there. He's my son in law's step-brother-in-law. We live up to the stereotype, don't we?"

"I'm not related, and they all feel like family to me. I love that about this town."

"You *are* family to Kiley. And little Diana lights up every time she sees you. I've got a lot to make up for with my girls. So, I wanted to give you a heads-up."

She was still puzzled, but she thought she saw something in Jack she hadn't before. Maybe he really was trying to be a better person. Maybe they weren't so different, the two of them.

And then he brought his head up real slow, looked right into her eyes. "This guy who's on his way here, his name's Braxton Hayes."

Everything in her—body, blood, breath, bone—spun into a whirlpool that had opened under her feet. She was clawing to hold onto the edges, to keep from falling into the dark vortex. And she did it. She held on, palms flat to the counter. No more than a second had passed. Jack might've noticed. He might not. Hell, he might already know.

It had been a long, long time since she'd heard her brother's name. And Jack Kellogg, alleged master of the con, not long out of prison, felt compelled to walk in here and tell her that Brax was coming for her just like she'd always known he would.

"Thanks for the cookies," Jack said, all easy and smooth, like he didn't know that he'd just set her world on fire. Trying to read his face was a waste of time. It only showed what he wanted her to see. Schoolboy dimples and mischievous Newman-blue eyes. "So long, Sunny. You take care, now."

He was out the door before she'd regained the power of speech. She closed her eyes. Opened them again. She wanted to believe it was coincidence, that Jack had just come in here and spilled his guts to her like a drinker to a bartender. Instead of alcohol, she served sugar. And weren't they sort of the same thing?

But no. It had been no accident. Jack had walked in to warn her, and that meant he knew.

And if he knew, her life in Big Falls was over.

"Oh, no," she whispered. "Oh no."

CHAPTER 3

*S*unny knew the plan by heart. If anyone mentioned her real name, or her father or her brother or the Barrier Park Protest, she was to call Eve immediately.

She also knew what Eve would say.

It was good that Jason was coming over to end things between them. He wanted more and he'd finally run out of patience. It was good. He deserved someone who could be his wife, raise kids with him.

Her throat tightened up so much it hurt. It would be hard for him to tell her it was over. He was kind right to his bones. Maybe she should beat him to the punch. Break up with him first. Let him off the hook, so he wouldn't feel guilty later on, especially if something should happen to her.

She had to call Eve. That was first. Eve had drummed it into her head like a jack hammer. She could hear her inside her brain, as if she were standing there saying it out loud. "Anything looks off, first thing you do is call me. If a freaking chipmunk looks at you funny, you call me. That's the first thing you do. You got it?"

So that's what she did as soon as she'd locked up behind Jack.

She tapped "Eve," in her phone's contacts and it dialed the number she knew by heart. It went to voicemail. The recording said it was safe to leave a message. She didn't trust that for a minute. They hacked something new every day. They'd hacked anti-hacking service, for crying out loud.

The tone beeped. She said, "Someone with a shady past just casually let me know my brother is on his way here. Safe to say he knows who I am, but I don't–" She had to swallow hard before she could continue. "I don't want to go," she whispered. "I don't want to leave my life here. So, call me."

She put down the phone and picked up her head. She had to bull through this, do whatever was necessary. Just like before.

She took a deep breath and put all her focus on getting ready. If this was going to be the last time she saw Jason McIntyre, she wanted to look her best. Light blue sundress, and strappy straw-yellow sandals. She wanted him to remember her just the way he knew her. Even though it was a lie.

Jason took pains with his appearance. He wanted to look nice when he asked Sunny the big question. And then he wondered if he thought that would change the outcome. She wasn't going to get excited or tear up with joy. She was going feel cornered, forced into making a choice she didn't want to make.

Maybe he shouldn't ask her yet. Maybe he should just tell her how he felt, instead, and insist she listen for once, and save the whole down-on-one-knee thing for a time when she'd be happy about it. A proposal shouldn't be an ultimatum.

He picked out a nice bottle of wine and thought about flowers, too, but decided against them. If she saw him coming with wine *and* flowers, she'd sense what he was up to, or at least pick up its general direction, and she'd be out of there before he could get a word out. She'd invent an emergency or stub her toe, or remember she'd left the oven on–anything to avoid having the conversation. Just like she'd done before.

So just the wine.

He glanced at the bottle as he exited Main Street Liquor & Cigars. Lucy and Mike "Chappie" Chapwell, the owners, watched him all the way back to his truck, and he was sure they were still watching when he pulled into Sunny's, across the street and three doors down. Half this town was waiting for him and Sunny to announce their engagement. Not to mention his family, every step- and half- and in-law member of it.

He closed his hand around the box in his jacket pocket and said a little prayer for luck.

The pink and white awning of Sunny's Place stood out from the rest of the shops with their green and white stripes. Kind of like Sunny stood out from other women.

Taking a deep breath, he got out and walked around back. He didn't go to the door, but across the back lawn, and onto a well-worn downhill path to the Cimarron. Sunny's riverside gazebo came into view. It was a white octagon, Amish-built, with four wide steps at the front. Its elevation improved the view, Sunny had said when she'd supervised the setup of it. It was surrounded by boulders she'd picked out herself. They had to be the right colors, to match the rocks along the riverbanks. Red and brown and rusty.

The pavilion had built-in benches with pretty pillows and a glass-topped table. Sunny had tied long white swatches of sheer fabric to each of its eight pillar posts, and they danced in the river breeze while the chimes hanging in between tinkled magically. It was her princess castle, she said, and her favorite spot in the world.

It was the best place to have this conversation. She'd be relaxed and happy and blissful in her special place, a little more amenable to romantic declarations and planning a future.

He strained to see inside as he walked down the path, wine

bottle in hand, but it was shadowy. It got dark early in February. Valentine's Day was right around the corner. Maybe he should've waited to pop the question until then.

She came to the side and waved at him over the railing, and he waved back. Hell, he didn't know if he could do this. What if she said no?

∾

Sunny had brought a bucket of ice and a couple of wine glasses and walked down to the pavilion. He'd texted he was bringing wine. Twice, she'd slipped on the trail and almost dropped her ice bucket. It had rained that afternoon, and everything was slick and damp and shiny. It smelled good outside. Clean and fresh. It wouldn't last long.

The pavilion was her very favorite place. She'd set the ice bucket on the little table, and moved to the open end facing the river to watch the water and wait for Jason. The Cimarron was wide and lazy there, and watching the water snaking over itself was soothing.

God, she was going to miss this place. This rolling river, her princess pavilion, the bakery. Jason. She'd thought their inevitable ending would hurt less if she didn't let it go too far. So why did it feel like being turned inside out? She closed her eyes, and they felt hot, and she tried to focus on the music around her. The river's song, the breeze, the chimes jingling magically and... there. That was better. She opened her eyes again.

Jason was coming down the path, the promised wine in hand. God, he looked good. This was going to be a hard day. The hardest one in six years. The hardest one ever. But her brother was coming. And anyone close to her would be in his crosshairs.

For an instant, she felt Dave's warm blood on her blouse,

sticky on her skin, but she shook the memory away hard and pulled her mouth into a welcoming smile.

Jason jogged up the pavilion steps, gave her a one-armed hug, and a kiss on the cheek. "You're beautiful, as always."

"Thank you. You always say the nicest things." She took the wine from him and turned to put the bottle into the ice bucket. She twisted it deeper, then went around the little table and sat on the white wicker sofa with the fat floral cushions.

Jason stood for a minute, kind of uneasily shifting his weight back and forth. She decided to let him off the hook. This was going to be too hard on him. "It's okay. It really is." She pulled the bottle back out, and made quick work of opening it.

"It's already chilled. I had Chappie put it on ice ahead of time."

"That was good thinking." She filled both glasses way more than was fashionable, and dropped the bottle back into the ice, uncorked. Then she took her glass and drank it halfway down. "I think we both know we're at a fork in the road."

His brows went up, like he was surprised she'd brought it up first. "I didn't think you were feeling that as much as I was."

"I am. I know you want more, Jason. Your brothers are all married with kids, and I know that's how you see our future."

His breath rushed out of him. "Our future," he repeated, and then he bent down, picked up the little glass topped table and moved it three feet to the left, giving him room to drop onto one knee in front of her.

His knee touched down, and she sprang up as if one triggered the other. "I was beginning to think you didn't want a future with me at all," he said, pulling a little box from his pocket.

"Jason, don't. Get up, now." He frowned, but didn't get up. She turned and paced away from him. He couldn't propose if she moved out from in front of him, could he? "Geeze, I thought you were here to break up with me."

"Why would I break up with you? I want to marry you!"

"No, you don't!" She shouted it. "Jason, you don't even know me."

"How can you say that? I know you better than anybody."

"You think you do. But–"

He put the box back into his pocket, and she could feel his hurt.

"I know your favorite movie is *The Princess Bride*, and your favorite food is angel food cake with whipped cream frosting, drizzled in chocolate syrup, and that you hate people fussing over your birthday and would rather forget it. I know you love this town and everyone in it. I even know the parts you think you hide."

That statement made her look him square in the eye. He rose slowly. "You never talk about your past, your family. I see the shadows in your eyes sometimes. You have a history. You have secrets. That's okay with me. You'll tell me when you're ready."

"No, I won't."

"I know you idolize your mother." He moved closer, slid his hands over her elbows. "Your whole wardrobe seems inspired by that one photo you have of her on the little table in your living room. All those pastel sundresses and soft little sweaters, all the fake pearl necklaces, pink ones and lilac ones and robin's egg blue ones. Even your hair is like hers."

"Please don't." She turned away, even though she didn't want to. Tears burned behind her eyes.

"Sunny, I love you. I've loved you for a long time now, but I didn't think you really wanted to hear it."

A sob broke through. She'd been holding them back but this one was too big, and she choked on it.

He closed his hands on her shoulders. "Sunny, please don't cry. Being loved shouldn't be something to cry about."

Her face was wet, tears dripping off her jaw and rolling

down her neck, and her lungs kept spasming. "I can't be what you need, Jason."

"You already are what I need."

"No. No, you need a woman who can marry you, and be a mother to your children, and make you happy. And that's not me, Jason. It's not me, and I should've told you that a long time ago."

"Told me what? You...you don't want kids?"

"I can't be a mother. Or a wife. It's too big a commitment. I can't be sure I'd be able to–"

"Sunny what the hell is going on with you?"

Her back was to him. She saw the truck pull into the driveway and park beside Jason's. "That's Bernie Jennings to pick up the extras for the shelter. I have to go." She started to walk across the gazebo, but he got in front of her and blocked her path.

"No. Dammit, Sunny, we need to have this conversation. Bernie can wait a minute."

"Let me pass, Jason."

"Not until you give me an answer."

"The answer is no. And I'm pretty sure last time I checked, that's all the answer that's required. Now get out of my way." She shoved him hard, already regretting that she'd sounded so cold, just then. So cruel. He stumbled a little, reaching for her again, but she ducked his grasp intuitively, and lunged toward the stairs as if fleeing for her life. If she didn't get away from him soon, she'd crumble. Her foot slid across the rain wet top step as if it were made of ice, and she went over the railing headfirst. There was an explosion at the bottom, or at least that was how it felt inside her head. Pain, white hot, and a jolt that hammered down her spine to her toes.

∼

"Sunny!" Jason saw her fall. One foot slipped outward so fast its momentum carried the rest of her. She flipped right off that railing and cracked her head on the boulder at the bottom.

He ran to the steps, jumped the railing, vaguely aware of Bernie Jennings' shout and pounding footfalls coming down the path.

Sunny lay face up on the boulder like it was a giant pillow. Her eyes were closed and his heart tripped over itself. "It wasn't her head that hit, it wasn't her head—" He fell onto all fours on that boulder beside her, one hand on her face, but tentative.

"What were you thinking, Jason McIntyre?" Bernie was already tapping 911 into his phone as he reached the end of the path.

Jason ignored the other man, not even processing his words. He was looking at Sunny's head for signs of injury, but he didn't want to move her. And then he saw the blood spreading over the boulder from beneath her head, soaking her hair. He kept almost touching her, then pulling his hands away. "Sunny? Sunny, come on, please, wake up."

His phone was in his hand and he'd tapped his cousin Sophie's headshot before he knew he was doing it. Bernie was a dull murmur in the distance.

"You got Doc Sophie," she answered cheerfully.

"Sunny just fell off the pavilion and smashed her head on a boulder. She's unconscious. And bleeding."

"Jason?"

"It's bleeding, Soph! What do I do?"

"Don't move her. Heads bleed a lot, so it probably looks worse than it is." He heard footsteps, doors slamming around his cousin. She never stopped talking. "I'll be there in five. Pressure on the wound, but only if you can do it without moving her head or neck." He heard a car door, an engine starting. "I'll call nine-one-one on my way."

"Bernie's here, he's already on with them."

"Good. Put your phone down and focus on Sunny."

He hung up and put the phone back into his pocket, his fingertips brushing over the engagement ring box. It sent a sharp pain straight through his heart, and it hurt so much he couldn't think for a second. So, he snapped himself out of it by calculating Sophie's ETA. Two miles to her place, maybe a little less.

He tried to press his hand to Sunny's head, to apply pressure like Sophie had said, pressed his other hand flat to her cheek to keep her head and neck from turning and was still not pressing hard enough to stanch the flow. "Sunny, come on. Come on, wake up. Talk to me."

It was hard not to pull her into his arms and rock her, and apologize six ways to Sunday for pressuring her. He'd anticipated that she might say no. He had not expected her to flee in panic.

Sophie came bounding down the path, hollering at Bernie to go back up and wait for the ambulance. Then she moved Jason aside and took over.

He felt guilty as hell, wished he'd listened to his inner voice and not pushed her. Dammit, look what he'd done. What if she wasn't okay?

It was half torture, half relief when the EMTs joined Sophie, forcing Jason to step aside. He could only watch as they worked, two young locals, and his cousin Sophie. He had to move around to see between their bodies. They got a neck brace onto her, and then a backboard under her. Once she was strapped down, Sophie pressed sterile pads under her head and wrapped gauze around and under her chin to keep it there. Then she gave a nod, and the two guys carried her up the hill to the ambulance waiting on the back lawn. Bernie had moved his truck, but he waited at the top.

Sophie's hand fell on his shoulder. "I'm gonna ride along, just in case. You can bring my car or your truck. Your call."

"Truck," he grunted. "I'm used to it. Won't have to think."

"Okay."

"Is she gonna be okay, Sophie?"

"No way to tell you anything without some X-rays and a CT scan. Unless she comes to on the way." She let go of his shoulder and started up the path, and Jason hurried after her, looking back only once at Sunny's favorite spot.

The ice bucket sat on the little glass table, cubes melting. The open wine bottle rested inside, their glasses on the table. And the clay red boulder beside the pavilion was stained with Sunny's blood.

CHAPTER 4

J ason would've called her family if she had any. She
didn't. She'd been an only child. Her parents had
died in an avalanche while skiing the Swiss Alps
when she was just a baby. She'd been raised by a series of foster
parents since then. She was entirely on her own.

He'd always admired that she managed to be so happy and
well-adjusted even though she had no kin. Not that she didn't
have a dark side, she did. Everyone did. He'd been with her
three years before he'd seen her lose her temper. People being
mean to children or animals were a surefire way to set her off.
And man when she went, she *went*. He'd seen her capacity for
fury when a young mother had smacked her little toddler's
cheek at the grocery store. The look that had come into Sunny's
always-smiling eyes had given him a chill right to his bones.
She'd snatched the woman's wallet right out of her hand,
opened it, read her name aloud, handed it back and said, "I'll be
sure to spell it right when I call social services later."

Then she'd visibly caught hold of herself, schooled her
expression before she looked at him again, and walked out of

the store, leaving him to pay for their purchases while she waited in the car.

There was a temper in there. That had been his first glimpse of it, but he'd seen it once or twice since. She kept it carefully controlled and deeply buried. He had a theory that she had reason to. But she didn't talk about things like that.

He didn't know how she'd grown up without family. So much of who he was today had been shaped by life with his brothers on his parents' Texas estate. His mom still lived there with her second husband. His dad was with him still, here in Big Falls, and married to the widowed saloon owner Vidalia Brand.

Thinking of Vidalia reminded him of her notorious family text loop. Everyone was on it; her five daughters—one of whom was his half-sister—all their husbands, his own two brothers and sisters-in-law, and his dad. The loop was overused for mundane things, and often irritating because of that. You could silence it at night, and have seventy-five messages waiting in the morning, none of which had anything to do with anything.

This, however, was one of those rare occasions when he was damn glad of the loop's existence.

He texted the family. "Sunny fell. Hit her head. Tucker Lake ER."

The questions came pouring in after that. In a way, it was a relief. A distraction from the waiting.

Before another hour had passed, Joey had joined him in the waiting room. He'd brought pizza. Rob's wife Kiley showed up with her dad, Jack Kellogg, in tow. Kiley had tears shining on her freckles when she ran up and hugged him. She loved Sunny like a sister. "Is she okay? What happened? Did she jump before or after you popped the question?"

He blinked. "She didn't jump, she fell. And how do you even know about that?"

"We all know," Joey said. "And in case you didn't get the memo, Jay, if you tell a secret to one of us, you tell it to all of us."

"*I* didn't know," Jack said. "If that's any comfort."

Jason acknowledged Jack just to be polite. It was decent of him to come, but Jason didn't trust the guy.

"Rob and Dax are delivering a foal or they'd be here, too," Joey said.

"It's the roan," Kiley added. "She's having trouble. Dad thought I was too upset to drive myself, so he brought me."

"Emily's helping with the colt, so I came solo," Joey said. "She said it might be a while but not to worry. She's seen worse." Joey lifted the lid of the pizza box. "Have a slice, big brother. You'll feel better."

"I can't."

"So, what happened?" Kiley asked.

"Yeah, I was about to ask the same question." That was Jimmy Corona. He'd just entered the waiting room from the hallway, and he was in uniform, down to the hat and the badge. "Can we talk a minute in private, Jason?"

Jason got a little shiver right up his spine. "No need to be private, Jimmy. We're all family here."

"Yeah, um, this isn't a family kind of conversation."

"Why don't you just say what you mean, Chief Corona?" Kiley said. She crossed her arms over her chest and planted herself right in between Jason and Jimmy, the little freckle-faced warrior. Jimmy was family. Calling him Chief Corona had been a message, and he'd clearly received it.

"Damn, my brother married a hellion," Jason said. "Stand down, Kiley. Jimmy, we don't need privacy for this. I'll say it in front of everyone. I really messed up. This was my fault."

"Tell me everything that happened," Jimmy said. "Don't leave anything out. I'm gonna record it, so no one can put words in your mouth later on."

"Who'd wanna—"

"Here. Let's sit." Jimmy took a seat at a small round table in the waiting room, laid his tape recorder in front of him.

29

Sighing, Jason sat across from him. He took a deep breath. "We met in the pavilion. Drank a glass of wine. I asked her to marry me. She freaked out, stormed away, slipped on the top stop, fell and hit her head on the boulder."

"Okay," Jimmy said nodding. "But can you slow it down a little? Go step by step. You asked her to marry you and she freaked out, and then what happened? Physically, what happened? Where was she? Where were you? Who touched who—"

"Who touched who?" Jason stood up. "What the hell are you asking me, Jimmy?"

"Just tell it again. Slower. I need to have it down, okay?"

Jason closed his eyes, and called it all back into his mind. "She turned to leave me. She was upset. I went around in front of her, like to block her from the stairs. I told her she wasn't leaving until we finished talking. It was stupid. I was mad."

"Did you put your hands on her?"

"Of course not!" The words burst from him.

His brother Joey moved right up beside him, clamped his shoulder hard with one hand. "This is starting to sound like an interrogation, Jimmy. Should I call my brother a lawyer?"

"I don't need a lawyer."

"Then tell me the rest," Jimmy said.

"It's Bernie Jennings, isn't it? He was there, and I remember him saying something weird to me, but I was too worried about Sunny to pay any mind. What does he think he saw?"

"You first," Jimmy said. "Finish the story. You stepped in front of her and told her she couldn't leave."

"Right. Like a freaking caveman. She reminded me that 'no' is a complete answer, shoved me out of her way so hard I almost fell on my ass, which I richly deserved. Then she took two steps, hit the wet stairs and fell."

Jimmy nodded. "Now think real hard, Jason. When she shoved you, did you grab for her in any way?"

"I told you, I didn't touch her–"

"But did you reach for her?"

He frowned hard, thinking back. "I might've reached out for something to keep from falling, but I caught my balance." He tried to re-visualize in his mind exactly what he remembered. She'd shoved him sideways with both hands, hard. He'd gone stumbling to the left, and kind of flailed his arms right. She was already striding past him as he wobbled, caught his balance, righted himself.

"I supposed from a distance, it might've looked like I was reaching for her. I wasn't. I was trying to keep from falling."

"But you didn't touch her," Jimmy said.

"I didn't touch her. I've never touched a woman in anger in my life, nor would I. She just...fell. She just fell. I saw it happen and couldn't do a damn thing to stop it. She'll tell you the same thing herself, when she wakes up."

Sophie came into the waiting room, and he forgot everything else, surged out of his chair and went to her. "How is she? Is she okay?"

His cousin nodded slowly. "I think she will be," she said, and everyone in the room sighed in relief. "She's stable for now."

She had more to say, but hesitated and Jason thought he knew why. "You can't tell me more. We're not family. Not legally."

"You're her health proxy," she said.

"I had no idea."

"She filed it in my office last year. Just in case, she said. So, I can discuss this with you. But everyone else—"

"You'll fill us in," Kiley told him.

It didn't feel like a question. "Yeah. Sure, I will. You and Angie are her best friends–shoot, someone should call Angie!"

"I already did," Kiley said. "Go on with Sophie, and then get back here so we know she's okay."

He nodded and looked at Jimmy.

"Go on," Jimmy said. "I'll hang around until I can talk to her, so she can set the record straight."

"Okay."

Sophie took his arm and guided him out into the hall, across it and around a corner, talking as they went. "She's still unconscious. There's no skull fracture, no visible damage to her brain. We'll watch her closely in case of swelling and wait for her to wake up. We're not gonna know much more until she does."

He followed her through a set of doors, around a corner and, finally, into a room. Sunny lay in the bed. There was a big white patch on the upper left side of her head, right behind her ear, and there was no hair around its edges.

"You shaved her head? She's not gonna like that, Soph."

"Yeah, she's not gonna like this either. And I could probably lose my job for showing you, but you're family. Family comes first. And this is...this is something you need to know about." She shook her head slow.

"What are you talking about?"

She moved up beside the bed and peeled back the bandage.

There, tattooed onto the scalp of the sweetest, kindest, sunniest gal in Big Falls, the girl whose personality matched her name, was a swastika.

"What the...who...how did that get there?"

"Well, don't look at me, I don't know how to make a prison tattoo, but that's what it looks like. Amateur, blue ink, a real hack job."

"Why would Sunny have a tattoo like that? Sunny? Of all people?"

Sophie shook her head slowly. "I don't know, Jason. I don't know, but maybe it's a good thing your proposal got interrupted."

~

32

Age 15

Mary was still flush with excitement when she sailed through the front door at 9 p.m. She could not believe what had happened to her that day. Things like that just didn't happen to girls like her.

"What the hell are you smiling about? You know what time it is?"

That was her father's greeting. Like ice water thrown on the warmth that had been suffusing her entire being. "I put on a crockpot of chili this morning. Extra spicy. And there's still a full loaf of the bread I baked over the weekend. Wasn't it all right?"

"I'm gettin' sick of crock pot food. When is stupid softball season over, anyway?" Brax whined.

She'd been playing for five seasons. He knew the schedule as well as she did. "I pitched a no-hitter today," she said. She was a freshman, and this was her second year on the varsity team. They were saying she was the youngest pitcher ever to throw a no-hitter, male or female.

"Well, aren't you special?" That was her dad.

"We made it to the sectionals. I'm starting pitcher from now on."

"At least that's something to be proud of." Almost before she could feel surprised at her father's rare praise, he ruined it. "The previous starting pitcher was a black girl, wasn't she? Good you put her in her place. Just don't forget yours."

She didn't know how her father knew who the starting pitcher had been before her, and she didn't bother telling her dad that Gemma had busted her wrist earlier in the season. The catcher tried to throw down on a runner stealing second. Gemma forgot to duck and got hit.

She was a good pitcher. And a nice person. People seemed to like her, but Mary wasn't allowed to talk or socialize with what her father called the impure races. Which was like, half her school. Seemed to her like most of the planet.

Life was easier when she obeyed without question. It hadn't ever occurred to her to question her father's take on things until high school. Now it seemed to be happening more and more frequently. She got into trouble every time, too.

"We have a rally tonight," her dad said.

"I'm kind of tired. Maybe I could skip this one?"

"You're the Grand Exalted Nighthawk's daughter. No, you can *not* skip this one. Mouthy little bitch."

Yeah, she thought, Grand Exalted Nighthawk, a made-up title for his made-up group of eighteen, most of them related. But she didn't speak her thoughts out loud or even mutter them under her breath. Obedience was always the safest course.

"And we're out of cookies. You've got an hour."

Cookies for eighteen pigs in an hour's time, she thought. No problem. She was good at this. She whipped up a quick batch of big, soft sugar cookies with a hint of orange zest and sugar sprinkles. While each batch baked, she hurried through a shower, put on fresh clothes, including a worn-out white pride T-shirt, and loaded up the tiki torches and cardboard signs.

CHAPTER 5

Sunny came around slowly, like swimming to the surface from cold, deep water. She felt pain in her head, a familiar pain. She'd felt it before, and for one brief moment she was reliving the most terrifying moments of her life, fighting to escape, held down, hurting.

And then she realized all that had been long ago. She was in Big Falls. She was lying on her side in a strange bed, facing a white wall with white curtains. The bedside stand, the tray table —she was in a hospital. How odd.

There was a gentle touch on the sore spot of her head. Then Jason's voice. "How did that get there?"

"Well, don't look at me." She knew that voice, too. Doc Sophie, Jason's cousin. "I don't know how to make prison tattoos, but that's what it looks like. Amateur, a real hack-job."

"Why would Sunny have a tattoo like that? Sunny? Of all people?"

Oh, God, they'd seen the tattoo. Her most shameful secrets were being ripped out of hiding, exposed to the blinding sun while Jason looked on.

"I don't know, Jason. I don't know, but maybe it's a good

thing your proposal got interrupted, huh? I mean, this makes me wonder if any of us really know Sunny at all."

"You're wrong," Jason said. "I know her."

~

Jason couldn't leave the hospital. He couldn't. He sent the others home, and ate the cold pizza Joey had left behind, and paced the waiting room. He tried to watch some TV. He even went outside and walked around the parking lot for a while, looking at the stars and thinking about Sunny. He'd loved her. Thought she was the one he'd spend the rest of his life with. But now, everything was different. That faded blue hate symbol on her scalp looked like it had been there a while. The lines were rough, uneven and jogged wildly here and there. It was criss-crossed with scars. He didn't know what to think.

A woman with a creamed coffee complexion and pixie short platinum blond hair came into the waiting room, looked around, focused on him. He didn't know her. She wore a pale gray suit, narrow skirt, matching blazer, unbuttoned over a light blue blouse. Her shoes were light blue, too. She came right over to him.

"You must be Jason," she said. "I'm Eve DuVall." She extended a hand and he shook automatically. "How's Sunny doing?"

"She's still... I'm sorry, who are you?"

She sighed and let the bulging bag she was carrying slide off her shoulder, into a nearby chair. It was a quilted black and white bag, and it didn't match her outfit.

"I'm sorry," she said with an easy smile. "Sunny and I are old friends. We knew each other in college."

"She's never mentioned you." He shrugged. She'd never mentioned anything about her past, though, he thought.

"She wouldn't have, anyway. We fell out of touch after grad-uation. I'm afraid I let a lot of friendships lapse, and that's on me." She had eyes like Bambi. Big and brown with paintbrush lashes. "Anyway, I called her last night and told her I'd be passing this way. She said I should stop and visit. When I got to her place, some folks walking by the bakery said they'd heard she was in the hospital, so I rushed right over. What happened? Did someone—?"

"No one did anything. She fell." It was odd she'd jump to that conclusion, "It was an accident," he went on. Sunny hadn't mentioned a friend coming to visit. Then again, he'd pushed her right into the discussion he was so damned determined to have. No time for small talk. He was such an ass.

"Do you think—I mean, could I see her?"

"She's still unconscious," he said. "I don't understand it. Doc Sophie doesn't either. Her brain seems fine, the scans look like she should be awake and aware. They're calling in a neurologist."

Eve closed her eyes and snatched three tissues from the box on a nearby table. "Would it be okay if I just…sit with her for a few minutes?"

There hadn't been a McIntyre male born who could stand to see a woman cry. "Yeah, sure. I've been doing the same, on and off. Go ahead. It's around the corner, there, second door on the left."

"Thanks."

He watched her go. She scooped up her big bag on the way. Sunny's past had been as unknown, unmentioned, un-talked-about as if it had never happened. As if she'd been born, full-grown, in the bakery. Now, two things in one day. An ugly hate symbol inked into her skin long ago, and an old friend from college. Was that too weird to be coincidental, or was that ugly stain on Sunny's head making him crazy?

~

There was a nurse bustling around, fiddling with her tubes, taking her blood pressure, and just being an all-around pain in Sunny's backside. It was hard pretending to be unconscious when people were poking and prodding you.

The door opened, closed, and a soft and blessedly familiar voice said, "They said I could sit with her for a few minutes."

Eve. Thank God.

"I don't see what harm it can do," the nurse said. "Visiting hours ended hours ago, though. So just a little while, or I'll be in trouble." The soft pad of her rubber soles moved away, the door opened and closed again. And then Eve's hand came to Sunny's shoulder. "We're all alone, so if you're awake—"

Sunny opened her eyes. "I'm so glad to see you, Eve. They saw the tattoo. Sophie—Dr. McIntyre—she showed it to Jason!"

"She trying to steal him from you, or something?"

"She's his cousin," Sunny said. "It's a close family."

Eve leaned down and gave her a hug.

"Love the new hair," Sunny said, hugging back. "I've missed you."

"Me, too."

"What are we gonna do, Eve?"

"First, we have to get you out of this hospital."

"I'm ready right now. Give me a ride?"

"Not like that. People get all upset when you sign yourself out AMA. We don't need a fuss made. So...you're gonna wake up, and you're gonna pretend you don't know who you are, or who any of them are."

"Why would I do that?"

"Because you don't want to have to explain that tattoo, and it will buy us some time. You banged your head. Amnesia happens when you bang your head."

"On TV maybe."

"It's plausible." Eve shrugged. "And it'll give us some time and space to get you the hell out of here."

Sunny closed her eyes. "I don't want to go. I love it here, Eve. I love my life."

"You won't *have* a life if Braxton shows up. He's dropped off the radar, Sunny. We have no idea where he is. I was planning to contact you to warn you, but you called me first."

"You don't know he's here, though."

"And yet someone tipped you off that he was coming here, right after he dropped out of sight."

Hot tears welled up and Sunny closed her eyes to keep them in. "What if it's a false alarm? I've made a good life, here. This town, my bakery. Jason. My friends. What if I give it all up for nothing?" Sunny opened her eyes, looked into Eve's, and saw her wavering.

"Look, we can't skip town until they release you from the hospital anyway. I'll snoop around and see what I can find out. Who told you your brother was coming?"

"And ex-con ex-con." At her friend's frown, Sunny explained, "Ex-con*vict* and ex-con *artist*. Allegedly ex, that is. He's my friend Kiley's dad, Jack."

Eve said, "Jack Kellogg," without inflection.

Sunny was surprised. "You know him?"

"We've...crossed paths." She cleared her throat and went to look out the window. "I've requested a field agent from the Oklahoma City Bureau to watch your room while you're here, just in case."

"You think no one's gonna notice that?"

"You'd rather I let your brother walk in here and kill you then?" she asked. Then, "Shhsh. Nurse."

Sunny closed her eyes fast, going limp, and Eve said, "Nurse, I think she might be starting to come around." The nurse came closer, and Eve pinched her arm. Sunny moved her head on the pillow and moaned a little.

"Dr. McIntyre was just at the desk," the nurse said. "I'll catch her." And she hurried out of the room.

Eve leaned down. "Amnesia, Sunny. Got it?"

She nodded very slightly. "It's ridiculous. No one will believe it." Then quickly added, "If I'm here overnight, make sure someone feeds my cat!"

The door burst open and people came in, the nurse, Sophie, and then she heard Jason's voice, and felt meaner than mean for what she was about to put the poor man through. He didn't deserve this. He didn't deserve any of this.

What was wrong with her, thinking she'd left the past behind? It would never be behind her, not ever.

"Sunny, can you hear me? Sunny?" Sophie pushed her eyelid up, and Sunny twisted her head away, then blinked rapidly. Then she looked around as if for the first time, trying to feign confusion, but when her gaze fell on Jason's, she couldn't look away. The relief on his face was intense. But she forced her own expression to stay blank.

Sophie said, "Do you remember what happened, Sunny?"

She frowned, avoiding all eyes, and whispered, "Who's Sunny?"

Sophie was so startled she backed up a step. Then she turned to Eve and Jason, and said, "I need you two to go on back to the waiting room."

"No." Jason crowded nearer the bed. He clasped Sunny's hand and looked her right in the eyes. "*You're* Sunny. You fell and hit your head, but you're okay now. You're okay now. Come on, Sunny."

"I...don't know who you are." Her heart broke into tinier pieces with every word. "I'm sorry. I don't...I don't know who *I* am." She sat up in the bed, Jason hurrying to help her. "I can't... why can't I remember anything?" she asked, sending her plea to Doc Sophie.

"You've been unconscious for hours. You're just confused is all," Sophie said. Her voice was clam and level, just about as reassuring as a voice could get. "Things will fall back into place in a little while. You're going to be all right. Just relax and give yourself time. You're safe. You're well. And you're going to be okay, that's all you need to think about right now." Then she turned, "Jason and um...I'm sorry–"

"Eve," Eve said. "Come on, Jason. Let's give the professionals some room." She touched his shoulder from behind, but he was leaning over Sunny, looking her over as if he was already doubting that her amnesia was for real. But he softened his eyes, touched her face with his fingertips. "You're gonna be okay, you hear?"

She nodded at him while her heart shredded itself. He took a deep breath, searched her eyes one last time, probably looking for some spark of recognition in them. Finally, he turned and left the room. Eve walked out beside him, one hand on his shoulder.

And then Sophie was back, asking her a hundred questions and shining that light into her eyes again. She tried to count to ten before answering every single one, thinking carefully before uttering a word. She hated this, hated lying to Sophie, hated lying to Jason even more.

"Well, I never thought I'd be saying this, but she seems to have amnesia."

Jason looked at his cousin as if she'd lapsed into Swahili. "Amnesia? Is that even real?"

"It's rare, but it does happen. Look, I'd already called in a neurologist when she failed to regain consciousness for so long. She'll be here in a couple of hours and she'll obviously have a lot more insight into this than I do." She squeezed his shoulder and said, "Jason, hon, you've been here all night. You need to go home. She's not gonna miss you being here, not in this condi- tion. Shower up, get a decent meal and a few hours of sleep.

Come back after lunch and I should have some more information for you. Okay?"

"Yeah," he said, lowering his head and rubbing the back of his neck with one hand. "Yeah, I'll go. I gotta fill the family in anyway. The text loop is probably exploding. I had to turn it off."

"A hundred and some odd messages since everyone left. Everyone but her, I mean."

He looked over at Eve, who sat in the far corner of the waiting room where tapping on her cell phone.

She caught him looking, pocketed the phone and came over as Sophie left them.

"What did the doctor say?"

"Sunny has amnesia, and no I'm not making this up. It's probably temporary. There's a neurologist coming to examine her soon and we'll know more then."

"Amnesia? I didn't think that really happened."

"Sophie says it's rare, but it happens."

"And what do you think?"

He opted not to answer that. "Do you have a place to stay in town, Eve?"

"I thought I'd probably spend the night with Sunny."

"My brother's saloon has rooms upstairs." The elevator doors opened. A guy in a suit glanced at Eve as he got out, and she met his eyes for a second before stepping in.

Jason got in and hit the G-button. The doors closed.

"Saloon?" she asked.

"The Long Branch. *Gunsmoke*-themed tourist hot spot, complete with fake shootouts and a player piano. Nothing rowdy, but it is busy. If you'd like something quieter, there's Ida Mae Peabody's Bed and Breakfast."

She smiled at him, and it lit her up. "I think The Long Branch sounds perfect. Thank you, Jason." The elevator doors slid open, and they walked down the hall to the exit.

"You can follow me back if you want. What are you driving?" he asked.

She wiggled her brows at him. "A-8." She tapped her keyring and he followed the flash of the headlights, then gave a long slow whistle. "How about you?" she asked.

"I'm in the F-150 parked cockeyed over yonder." He nodded toward his truck. "I was in a hurry."

"I bet you were." She stared at him a second, then sighed like she was sad about something, put her head down and headed for her car.

He got behind the wheel of his pickup and gave her time to pull up behind him before leaving the parking lot.

They gave her something to help her sleep, but she wished they hadn't. It just made her dream, and ever since she'd heard her brother's name, her dreams had become memories, buried for years, but never dead.

It was the end of her senior year. She'd had the letter for two weeks, and had finally worked up the nerve to show him.

He read the paper, made a disgusted face and crumpled it.

"It's a full scholarship, Dad. They want me to pitch for State. They'll even give me extra for books and a meal plan."

He'd been in the back yard, spray painting racial slurs on plywood squares. Plywood signs lasted longer, he said. And you could hit counter protestors with them. "Girls only go to college to get married. And no daughter of mine is gonna wind up hitched to liberal college boy."

"Girls go to college for all kinds of things today, Dad."

"No."

"But I could learn a trade, help support you when you get older."

"That's what I had a son for."

43

She'd been afraid that would be his answer. She had to accept the scholarship and register before the deadline passed, and she wouldn't be eighteen until after. She needed his signature, and his permission.

"I said no."

She remembered the hurt of that. The disappointment. But then something else came to her, and it felt like the culmination of all those times she'd disagreed with his philosophies or his rules and squelched it to avoid the back of his hand.

It all bubbled up in her.

She picked up the crumpled sheets from the ground, took them back to her room, smoothed them out, and signed his name on them. She could sneak out long enough to register for classes. And she'd be eighteen by the time August rolled around and they started.

She'd defied him for the first of time that day. She'd taken the first step toward Dave Barron's death sentence. And eventually, her own. But she hadn't known at the time just how bad her father's vengeance would be.

CHAPTER 6

$\mathcal{S}$unny's long, tall Texan led Eve in through a set of actual swinging doors–what did they call them? Bat wings. Something like that. It was almost two, and only a few customers lingered in the bar. Jason put one hand on her upper arm, like she was too delicate to wend her way through the saloon without his help. She moved it away. "I'm good."

He glanced at her with puzzled eyes. Then his brows went up and he said, "Sorry." He kept his paws to himself and walked up to the bar, but waited for her to sit first. Eve noted the saddle-shaped stool she'd have to straddle and said, "I'll stand, thanks."

The bartender came over and she wondered if every man in this town had Hemsworth DNA.

"Joey, this is Eve uh..."

"DuVall," she said.

"Right. She's a friend of Sunny's. Eve, this is my brother, Joe."

"Brother," she repeated, stretching out the word. "That explains it."

"Explains what?" Joey asked.

45

MAGGIE SHAYNE

She just shook her head and glanced at the stairs. "I'm told you have rooms up there."

"Sure do." He reached under the counter for a key, and said, "The corner's vacant. Best room in the place."

"Sounds above my pay grade. I just need a bed and a bathroom."

"It's on the house. Sunny is family, so any friend of hers is family, too. I'm glad you're here for her. Anything you need, you just holler." He slid the key across the bar. "And, for you, big brother," he added, pulling an envelope from his back pocket and passing it around to Jason. "Matilda Louise made Sunny a get-well card. Em helped with the spelling." Then with a smile her way, he clarified. "Matilda's my little girl. Emily's my everything else."

Eve tilted her head to one side in the way she might do if a unicorn had just walked up to the bar and ordered a beer. These guys were not dicks. They were genuinely decent. Would wonders never cease?

"Thank you. That's...unexpected."

"No problem."

Eve took the key and headed up the stairs, and Joe called after her, "Hang a right. It's number four."

She followed instructions, inserted the key, opened the door and stepped into her room, which continued the old western theme of the rest of the place. Antique washstand with pitcher and bowl, hurricane style lamps, wagon wheel light fixture and headboard. There was a second room, with a Victorian settee, and a shaker hutch that probably held a TV. Lace doilies, and old tin type photos of cowboys with long mustaches and dusty chaps. There was even a framed photo collage of Big Falls from days gone by, with muddy roads and horses pulling buggies and wagons.

"Wow. This place is something else."

She hadn't been there before. All her work setting things up for Sunny had been done remotely. The internet was the greatest invention of all time, no question. She put down her bag, took out a change of clothes, her phone and her gun, and then she hit the shower.

Not ten minutes later, someone was knocking at her door.

"Son of a—" She finished rinsing her hair, and jumped out, stubbed her toe, grabbed a towel, and hopped on one foot to open the bathroom door and shout, "Gimme a minute!"

Then she slammed it again, toweled off, and put on the complimentary bathrobe. It was nice, weighty like a spa robe, beige like one, too, and it had a longhorn skull and the words "The Long Branch" and "Big Falls OK" embroidered on the upper left chest.

It got stuck on her wet arms, and she wrestled with it, tied the sash and yanked it hard. She was not smiling when she finally opened the door.

Jack Kellogg stood on the other side, smiling down at her. "Hello, Evie. Long time, no see. Still with the FBI?"

"Shsh!" She grabbed him by the shirt, jerked him inside, and closed the door behind him. "What the hell, Jack? How did you even know I was here?"

"You would not believe the efficiency of the family grapevine. See, my daughter Kiley is married to Jason's brother Rob—"

"I've memorized the family tree."

He pulled a bottle of high-end vodka from behind his back. "Look what I brought."

"You steal that when Bartender Joe wasn't looking?"

He just wiggled his brows and walked to the old hutch, opened the front to reveal a mini fridge with a big bin full of ice in a tiny freezer compartment up top, and several soft drinks down below. There were glasses right beside it.

"I know who Sunny is," he said. "I did time with her old man.

And her brother, too, the little asshole." He dropped ice cubes into the glasses, then he poured.

"Are you the one who tipped him off that she was here?"

He handed her a glass. "I'm the one who tipped *her* off that he was coming."

"And who tipped *you* off that he was coming?"

"I still have contacts. They had no idea why Braxton Hayes and his inner circle of knuckle-draggers were on their way to my peaceful country town. They figured he must be looking for me, since I'm the only criminal here. You know, as far as anyone knows."

"Besides your daughters, you mean."

"Ah, yeah. Kiley never really was. I mean she tried, but my God, if there was a worse grifter, I never met her."

"And Kendra."

"Kendra was freaking amazing. But alas, she threw it all away for a man. Both daughters are well and truly reformed." He shrugged one shoulder. "Kendra still has grifter in her heart and soul, though. But still, reformed."

"So are you, I hear."

He lifted his glass. "I'm a grandpa now."

"Congratufuckin'lations." She downed the vodka, set down the glass. "Who told you Braxton Hayes was coming here?"

"Not gonna tell you that. Next question?"

"Has he arrived yet?"

"No."

"You know when he will?"

"No."

"Have you told anyone what you know about Sunny?"

"No."

"You plan to?"

"Well, never say never." She swung at him, he caught her wrist, their eyes locked, and then she leaned up and kissed the bastard. It was an impish little impulse that had come on too quick to resist. She kissed him hard, and when he started to go all soft, she jerked away fast.

"Why did you warn her?"

He turned away from her and took a leisurely sip from his glass. "Wanted to see what would happen. Didn't expect her to take a nosedive onto a boulder. How is she?"

"Amnesia," she said, deadpan.

"Bullshit," he said back.

She took his drink. "Get out, Jack." He gave her an "it's your loss" look, reached behind him to open the door and backed out with a little bow.

Eve swallowed the rest of her drink, set the glass down, and said, "I've got to get Sunny the hell out of this town."

Jason went to Sunny's to make sure it was locked up and feed the cat.

Griselda, Griz for short, hated Jason's guts. She wouldn't let him pet her, but often hid around corners to ambush him as he passed. She'd wrap around his shin and do her best to claw and bite him right through his jeans, yowling angrily the entire time.

He pulled around to the back, and took the outside stairs up. Sunny lived in the entire second floor of the building, while her bakery took up the ground floor. The exterior stairs zig-zagged up the back to her door. He used his key, watching carefully for the cat, slipped inside and closed it behind him. "Yo, Griz. You here?"

Nothing.

"Kitty kitty?" There was no reply so he went to the cabinet where Sunny stored the cat food and pulled down both a box and a can. The dishes were on the floor, empty and dry. He picked them up, rinsed and wiped them with a paper towel, then filled them. One with water, one with the single-serving can of cat food, and the third with a handful of dry kitty kibble.

"Roooooow!" Jason heard the cat a moment before she came galloping into the kitchen, skidding to a cartoon stop when she saw him standing there instead of Sunny.

"I'm not happy about it either, cat. But it is what it is."

She sat down and stared at him. If pressed, he'd have called it a death stare.

"Yeah, I know. But look here." He took the three dishes off the counter, and set them in their three-dish holder of wrought iron and filigree on the floor. The cat was slightly spoiled.

Griz stood up, leaned forward, then looked at him, and her narrow eyes seemed to ask, "What sort of trap have you set for me, human?"

"I'm just gonna ease on past you, okay?"

He moved as far to the right as the wall would allow and sidestepped past the cat, just trying to get out from between Griz and her bowl. She took a mighty swipe at him as he passed, but it was half-hearted. Her eyes were on the food. Griz liked food more than she liked much of anything.

Once he was out of her way, Griz trotted to the dishes, high-stepping like a Lipizzaner and digging in.

He should've rinsed the can, he thought. He shouldn't leave it in the sink like that. But he wasn't walking by her again so he'd just wait until she finished. He stood there, looking around the place he'd visited a few thousand times. He slept here sometimes. He showered here sometimes. He felt at home here. He probably shouldn't. Not with things the way they were at the moment, anyway.

The place was just like always. Mostly neat (not counting the cat hair) and pretty. There was a framed photo of the two of them taken last Christmas at the Long Branch's annual Christmas Tree Lighting and Sing-Along. It stood on the end table beside the sofa. A lump came into his throat. The photo beside it looked so much like Sunny it made him tear up. It was her mother, the only photo she had of her, she'd told him. Their eyes were so alike, and Sunny had that same curve to her cheeks. He picked the photo up. The glass jiggled in the frame, the photo inside sliding around loosely enough that he glimpsed another picture behind it.

And he was curious.

He knew better than to be snooping, but damn, things were weird with Sunny all of the sudden. And if she had amnesia, he had smallpox. Not to mention, she had a swastika tattooed to her head. And with that half-assed justification, he slid the back off the frame. He picked up the hidden photograph, which had "Hayes Family" written on it in ink.

He turned it over and looked at Sunny's mother, standing in the crook of a smiling, handsome man's arm. The man cradled a newborn in his other arm. The baby was wrapped in a blue blanket and wearing a blue cap, and his face was red and wrinkled. But what had his attention was the little girl. She stood in front of her parents, her mother's hands were on her shoulders. And from the shape of her nose to the smile in her eyes as she gazed adoringly at the newborn, he recognized her. Sunny. This was Sunny. Sunny, who'd told him she was an only child, and that her parents had died when she was a baby.

She was not a baby in the photo. She was three, maybe four years old.

He sank onto the sofa. All these pieces were spinning around in his brain and clicking into place one by one. Sunny had a history she didn't want him—or anyone—to know about. She'd been lying to him. All these years.

His head was spinning, but he put the photo back just the way he'd found it, wondering how Sunny got to be a Cantrell if her family's name was Hayes.

Had she been married, too? Was that another secret from Sunny's past?

Griz gave a little chuff-like sound, drawing his eye. She sat in the space between kitchen and living room, licking a paw daintily.

"You're welcome." He went past her, and she didn't even try to grab him, just kept him under surveillance as he rinsed the cat food can.

He topped off the water dish, refilled both food dishes. "In case you get hungry tonight," he said. And then he rinsed the cans and checked to be sure all the doors and windows were locked, and the heat was turned down, and the litter box was scooped, and nothing was plugged in, turned on or running that shouldn't be. And then he left, locking the door behind him.

Griz actually mewed at him, like she didn't want him to go.

"You know who that guy lurking around the floor is?" Doc Sophie asked the next morning. She stood beside the bed, skimming Sunny's chart,

"I don't know who anybody is, remember?" The neurologist had come and gone, spending less time with her than it would take to diagnose a pimple.

"Well, he seems to be interested in your room, so I thought you might have an idea." Sophie took her stethoscope from her pocket and cupped the business end with her hand to warm it. "I don't blame you if you're cranky. You want your life back. But the neurologist and I agree that this is likely to resolve itself in time."

"I just want to go home. Is there any medical reason for me to be here?"

"Not a one. You're being released today."

"That's fantastic. Thank you. That's…that's great."

"You um…you didn't ask how long."

She shrugged one shoulder. "You said today. I assume as soon as the paperwork's done—"

"Not how long 'til you can leave. How long until your memory will come back. You didn't ask."

She blinked. "I figured if you knew the answer to that, you'd have said so already."

She looked her in the eyes. "Sunny, you're not...faking this for some reason, are you?"

Sunny almost panicked. Her eyes widened, and then she quickly covered by blinking them fast and pressing a hand to her chest. "What a horrible thing to ask me!" She dropped her face into her palms.

"I'm sorry." The doc touched her shoulder, but Sunny jerked away, sniffled twice and said, "Just leave me alone."

"Okay. Listen, you have two visitors waiting out front. Angie and Kiley. They're your best friends."

They were. Angie had lost her husband in Afghanistan, and was raising two kids alone. And Kiley treated her like the sister she would never be. She couldn't lie to them.

"I can't. I...I really...I just can't." She lifted her head. "Sophie, please, please just ask them to leave. And don't tell them I'm being released. I need...I need some time."

"Okay. You sure you're all right?"

"Yeah. Just... Yeah. I'm gonna get dressed."

"I'll send a nurse in."

"I already hit the call button."

She nodded, frowned at her, but finally left her alone. Sunny peeled the tape off her forearm, and slid the IV clean out of her arm, then held pressure on the hole it left as she kicked her way out of the bed. She opened the little closet where her clothes were all stuffed in a giant plastic bag with handles and the words "Patient's Belongings" in blue across the front.

There were her things. She'd have preferred fresh ones, but she could get some at home. She just wanted to leave. Now.

She took her fingers off the IV hole in her arm and watched for bleeding. It turned dark red but didn't leak, so she ducked into the tiny bathroom to change. Her head was killing her, and there was barely room to bend over in the small restroom. There was a roll of adhesive tape, though. She ripped a small piece off with her teeth, and stuck it over the needle hole so she wouldn't bleed all over her clothes. That pale blue sundress.

Jason was right, when he said her wardrobe was inspired by that photo of her mother. And not just her wardrobe, her entire life. Everything about her was built around her mother, pieced together from a single photograph and faded, dusty memories.

She put on the blue sundress she'd chosen for Jason.

Jason. Oh, dammit, Jason. Tears welled in her eyes and spilled onto her cheeks. She didn't want to leave him.

But she didn't want him dead, either.

She looked at her reflection in the mirror. The big white patch on the side of her head was a welcome distraction. Jeeze, she couldn't walk around like that. She picked at the edges of the tape, got it loose, and peeled back the gauze pads. A long crooked row of black stitches cut diagonally across the swastika, adding a third set of arms to the thing. Maybe that changed its meaning somehow.

She folded the gauze into a smaller rectangle that just covered the wound, taped it on. Then she combed her hair all over to one side, covering the bandage, resulting in a one-eyed Jessica Rabbit sort of look.

She was still pushing it around on her head as she walked out of the little lav and right into Jason McIntyre's chest.

"There you are," he said, clasping her shoulders reflexively. "I was worried you'd skipped out on me."

She looked up at him, her gaze dancing all over his face because she couldn't look him in the eyes.

"Aww, Sunny, don't be so sad. You're gonna be okay. I promise."

She couldn't help but sink against him. She just couldn't stop herself. She leaned in, and turned her head and rested her cheek against his chest, and felt his heart beating. His arms closed around her, and his breath rushed out of him. She'd always loved the safe feeling she had when he wrapped her up against him. It was the only time she ever felt entirely safe. She spent every other second of her life waiting for an anvil to drop on her head. But not when Jason held her.

It felt better than it ever had, somehow. But it couldn't last. She couldn't stay. She lifted herself away from him eventually, stood straighter, forced her voice not to waver. "I'm sorry. This is all just overwhelming. What are you...what are you doing here?"

"Came to see you. Wanted to let you know your friend Eve is staying at the Long Branch. We'll take good care of her."

"Why didn't she just stay at my place?"

He looked at her, like he was seeing inside her brain, and she cleared her throat, went to her bed to straighten the covers, and added, "What's a Long Branch, anyway?"

He took a long time to answer. "My brother's saloon."

"Oh."

Silence stretched tight, and he finally broke it. "I brought you a card from Matilda Louise."

He was holding it out when she turned, a folded piece of green construction paper. She took it with hands that felt ice cold, unfolded it, and saw the six-year-old's crayon, glue and glitter artwork. There was a princess with a bandage on her head, and a little girl holding flowers.

She could not prevent hot tears from filling her eyes. "That's so sweet."

"She loves you."

"I love her, too." She bit her lip. "I mean, I must, right? How old is she?"

MAGGIE SHAYNE

"Six. She's my brother's little girl. Calls you Aunt Sunny even though we're not..." He shrugged, letting the words trail off.

She refolded the paper and held it, wishing she had a bag to put it in. "They're letting me go today," she said. "Just as soon as the paperwork's done."

"Perfect timing. I can give you a ride. That okay with you?"

She nodded. "I'd like that. Let me text Eve so she doesn't come all the way over here looking for me." She bit her lip. "The nurse says I'm from Big Falls, about an hour away."

"And what makes you think The Long Branch is in Big Falls?"

She didn't reply, just kicked herself mentally, went to the nightstand where she'd left her phone, and texted Eve. "Being released. Jason driving me home. Meet u there?"

"Absolutely."

She deleted the conversation, and pocketed the phone.

"You remember Eve, then." He said it like a statement, not a question.

"Yes, from yesterday. She was here when I first woke up."

"You knew her number was in your phone. Pulled it right up."

"She texted me earlier."

"She didn't mention she was staying at The Long Branch?"

"No, she didn't. I assumed she'd gone to my place." She finished her room search, finding nothing, because there was nothing to find, and faced him again. "I'm ready whenever you are."

"I thought you had to wait for paperwork."

"I don't want to wait. I want to go. Right now. Can we just go?"

"Yeah. Sure."

He kept a hand on her upper arm, like he always did. Like if she should stumble and fall, he'd be able to catch her. And she didn't doubt for a minute that he would. He was suspicious.

She'd known he would never fall for such a cliché. *Amnesia.* He wasn't an idiot.

He walked her out the door, down the hall, and she was sure someone would call out and stop them, but the nurses were all busy, and she was in civilian clothes, and looked like she knew where she was going.

They went through the double doors to the elevators, and he was helping her into his oversized truck before there was so much as a sign her absence had been noticed.

CHAPTER 7

*J*ason was 99% convinced Sunny's amnesia was a big fat lie. The problem was, Sunny Cantrell, the Sunny he knew, would never tell such a lie.

And yet she had. And she'd lied about other things, too, like when and how her family had died and being an only child. He'd tried to Google the Hayes family overnight, but it was such a common name that there were a few million results. He even tried Sunny Hayes, but there was no result at all on that search.

He was angry and hurt and worried about her. But he made small-talk on the ride from Tucker Lake to Big Falls all the same, mainly because he hadn't decided how to handle all this yet. And because she was fresh from the hospital, and while the amnesia might be phony, the thirteen stitches in her head were real enough.

She seemed interested in hearing him describe her life to her. He told her that her bakery was one of the most successful businesses in town, and how important it was to the community.

She looked surprised. "How is an ordinary bakery so important to Big Falls?" she asked as if she didn't believe him. Or maybe she wanted to be convinced.

"Are you kidding? Sunny's Place is the only bakery in town. You're a part of every baby shower, every graduation party, every wedding, and even most of the funerals. Big Falls wouldn't know what to do without you, Sunny."

"Without the bakery, you mean," she corrected.

"Without you," he countered.

He watched her a lot, looking for her expression to give away the truth. She'd slipped several times already. Tearing up over Matilda's card, knowing where the Long Branch was before he'd told her.

Falling into his arms, and resting her full length against him, like she always did when something was sad or scary or upsetting.

"Your apartment is on the second floor," he said, because describing her place some more would distract him from how bad he wanted her to break, and admit she was faking, and that she remembered him, and tell him what the hell was going on.

"Oh, is it?" Like she didn't already know. "What's it like?"

"Pretty and bright. Everything around you is pretty and bright, Sunny. Except for your cat."

"My cat?"

"Griselda. She's a hateful and vindictive harridan."

That made her smile.

"To everyone or just to you?"

"Mostly me. I think she just prefers your undivided attention." He sighed. "Poor thing's traumatized, being there alone."

"Poor Griz."

He hadn't said "Griz," he'd said "Griselda." Another strike against amnesia.

"It's right up here," he said. "The only building on Main Street with a pink and white awning. See?"

She nodded as he drove. Everyone who was outside waved

as they passed. Most of them already knew what had happened and where she'd been. Small towns were like that.

"I called over to Ida Mae's to tell Mickey—he works for you —not to open the bakery today. He said he'd let Tabitha, who also works for you, know." He spoke as the big truck rumbled into the driveway, and all the way to the back. "Think you can make the stairs?" he asked.

"Yeah. Aside from my head, I feel fine. Thank you for the ride." She opened the door and got out.

He did likewise, even though she hadn't asked. She started up the stairs, and he followed right behind. If she wanted him to go, he'd go, but he was waiting for her to tell him so.

At the top, she reached for her doorknob, and then froze in place, and he finally quit looking at her, and looked at the door instead.

"The door's open," she whispered.

"I made sure it was locked last night."

"What do you mean, last night?" she was looking at him wide-eyed.

"I came over to feed the cat. I have a key." As he said it, he noticed the pry marks on the door casing. He wedged himself between her and the door, forcing her back a few steps behind him. "Someone broke in. Go lock yourself in the truck and call Jimmy—Chief Corona. Just dial 911." He glanced behind him when she didn't move.

"Go on, be safe." He turned forward again, but she gripped his forearm like a bear trap snapping, and when he spun in surprise, the way she looked brought him to a standstill. Sheer terror, that was what was in her round eyes. Just sheer terror.

He grabbed her shoulders. "Hey, it's okay. The police station's right across the street."

"Then wait." She took out her phone, tugging him with her down a few more steps with her free hand. She had a death grip. "Hey, it's Sunny," she said, sounding very non-amnesiac.

"Someone broke into my apartment. I'm here with Jason, and he wants to go inside and I'm not gonna let him 'til someone gets here with a gun." She hung up immediately, and was texting one-handed while still pulling on his arm. He saw Eve's name over her shoulder.

They were tight, those two, and that didn't make sense. In all these years she'd never even mentioned Eve.

He let her pull him along until they were at the bottom. Jimmy Corona was already jogging across the street with one hand on his sidearm. He went past them up the stairs, pulled his gun, and went inside.

A few seconds later, he came back out. "No one's here. I'm going down to check the bakery." Then he went back in.

Sunny took that as permission to run up the stairs and into the apartment again, and before he caught up to her, she was inside, running around calling "kitty, kitty."

He closed the door behind him. Sunny was crawling on hands and knees, looking under the fat, colorful sofa and matching chair, looking for the cat she allegedly didn't remember.

"Griselda's not here," she said, sounding heartbroken. "She got out while the door was open."

"She goes outside all the time," he said. "She always comes back in short order. You've always told me she'd be miserable if she couldn't hunt."

Jimmy came back upstairs just as the unmistakable purr of the A8 told him Eve had arrived, as well. "Bakery's all clear," Jimmy said. "Nothing down there seems disturbed, it's still locked up. What about up here? Is there anything missing?"

He watched Sunny examine the room, saw where her gaze stopped and followed it. That photo of her mom was on the floor, its glass shattered. "Only my cat," she said. But there was more fear in her eyes.

"She wouldn't know if anything was missing, because she has amnesia. Right Sunny?" he asked. He willed her to look at him, to talk to him.

"Right," she said. "I wouldn't know."

"And she doesn't remember falling. So she can't tell you that I didn't push her, like Bernie Jennings thinks I did."

She shot him a horrified look. "I'm sure you didn't push me."

"But you don't remember. Right?"

She looked him in the eyes and tried to cover the fear in hers with some ice-cold emptiness. "I need you to go now, Jason."

He frowned hard, looking at her like she'd lost her mind. "Someone broke in here. I can't leave you alone—"

"I'm a grown woman. And Eve's here, and Jimmy's here, and I'm really sorry, but I want you to go." Tears tried to burn her eyes, but she willed them not to show.

There was hurt in his eyes, and a thousand questions, too. But he just said, "Okay. I guess I'll leave, then."

Sunny stood by the kitchen window and watched Jason all the way down to his truck. He looked up at her as he got in, and she ducked behind the curtain. Eve and Jimmy were talking in low voices in the living room.

"I think you might just be biased here, Chief Corona," Eve was saying. "You have a witness who says he pushed her."

"He didn't push me." She said it loud and firm.

"Well, you can tell us that with more conviction once you get your memory back," Eve said. "In the meantime, he's acting all stalkerish. How do you know it wasn't him in here last night?"

"He has a key. Why would he pry the door open?" Jimmy asked.

"Because if he used his key, we'd know it was him, Einstein. Look, I know he's your cousin or something, but you're the chief of police–"

"Step-brother-in-law. And I arrested his brother last year, so don't even think about accusing me of being biased."

"I'm not *accusing* you. If I accuse you, you'll know it!"

"Enough!" Sunny shouted. "Enough. Let's just...it's enough. I can't take any more. What am I–what are we doing? Just tell me what I'm supposed to be doing, all right?"

Eve nodded. "Pack an overnight bag. You can spend the night with me at the Long Branch. If that's okay with Chief Corona."

Jimmy gave Sunny a sympathetic nod. "Try not to touch any more than you have to. We need to go over the place for fingerprints and things." He slid a look at the broken photo frame on the floor.

Her family photo was behind the photo of her mother in the frame. She'd kept it only because it was the only other photo she had of her mother. She couldn't bear to throw it away, or cut it up, but she couldn't stand to look at the original either. So she kept it hidden, tucked behind the headshot of her mother.

Jimmy was going to find that photo, and then her secret would be out. And while she knew her life as Sunny Cantrell was over anyway, if Jason knew the truth he'd want to fix it. To save her. That was the kind of man he was.

And she couldn't let him take that risk.

God, when she'd seen the pry marks, and he'd started inside, she'd flashed back in time to Dave's broken body in her arms, his warm blood soaking her shirt. Only instead of Dave's lifeless eyes, it was Jason's she saw in their place.

She couldn't let that happen. "Check the bakery again, would you Jimmy? I think I left a bank bag with a few hundred in it under the register."

"Sure, Sunny."

As soon as he left, she went to the framed photo on the floor, and slid both images out of it. She shook the glass off her mother's face and turned to Eve. "Let's go."

"You in a hurry all the sudden?"

She nodded. "He's here, Eve. My brother is here. And no one's safe as long as that's true. He won't leave Big Falls until I do."

She and Eve left together in Eve's car while Jimmy was still downstairs checking for cash. But they didn't go far, just parked in the big lot behind the diner, where they could keep an eye on things. And when Chief Corona left her place, they walked back over there.

"Where's his crime scene crew?" Sunny asked Eve in a whisper as they started up the back steps once again. There was yellow tape across the top.

"Probably gonna be a while," Eve said. "Might even be morning. He thinks the place is secure and you're safe and sound. No reason for him to stick around."

They climbed over the tape and went inside. Eve closed all the curtains, and they used only minimal lighting. Sunny pulled suitcases out of her biggest closet. She started in the bedroom, quickly emptied her dresser into the case, and stuffed her jewelry box on top.

"We're gonna need a bigger boat." Eve stood in front of her open closet, eyeing rows of pastel dresses, blouses and skirts. The hooks in the wall held matching bags and the floor was lined with matching shoes.

"Leave all that," Sunny said softly.

"But—"

"That's Sunny Cantrell's stuff. I'm not her anymore. I don't know who I am right now. I'm in some kind of dark limbo waiting to find out, I guess. But I know I'm not her. I wanted to be. I tried to be." She went to the living room to get the framed photo of her and Jason off the end table, and brought it back to add to the suitcase on her bed. "But I was fooling myself."

MAGGIE SHAYNE

Eve closed the closet and came to the bed. She said, "You can be whoever you want to be."

"Obviously not. This is who I wanted to be. Sunny Cantrell, all sweetness and light, beloved of the best unmarried man in Oklahoma. And I pulled it off for a while. But in the end, my darkness just bubbled up and took it all away."

"It's your history that's dark, not you."

"I don't think so." Her eyes felt hot. She let the tears go. You couldn't hide a thing from Eve DuVall anyway.

"I'm sorry, Sunny." She really meant it, Sunny could tell, and then she tried to cheer her up by changing the subject. "Jimmy knew you remembered him. And so did Jason. You're terrible at this."

"I know I am. I totally forgot to pretend for a while there."

"Well, it was a shock, knowing he was in your place."

"What did he want here?"

"You. Either to find you and hurt you or to scare the hell out of you or to punish for your perceived sins. But he couldn't find you because you were in the hospital. Lucky break, banging your head like that."

A wave of fear rose up, but she pushed it down and went to the kitchen to start taking dishes out of the cupboards. "I have boxes downstairs," she said. "Newspapers, too, I think, to wrap the china."

"Hey, hey, wait a minute now. I didn't bring a moving van." Eve reached past her and closed the cupboard door. "And if we take everything, Chief Jimmy's gonna notice. We don't want anyone to know you're gone for as long as possible."

"Except my brother."

"What now?"

"Except my brother. We want him to know I'm gone."

"And just how are we gonna get a head start that way?"

"The longer he's in town, the more danger everyone is in. My friends. Jason. His family. The kids. Mouse and Tabitha."

66

"Who or what are Mouse and Tabitha?"

"They work for me."

Eve lowered her head. "I hate this for you, hon. I really do. I wish it could be different. But I'll get you your stuff, at least I can promise that. I'll have it all packed up and moved once your brother gives up and goes home. It can go in storage until you're settled in and ready for it. And then I'll send it on to you in your new place. Okay?"

"It's not like I have a choice." Sighing, she went to the bathroom and started packing up her personal things. Razors, toothbrush, makeup, hair products. She scooped them all into a plastic grocery bag and crammed that into the suitcase in the bedroom. "What am I gonna do about the bakery?"

"Leave word you're closing for the rest of the week to recover from your accident. Nobody's gonna question that. Not even Braxton. No matter who he asks or where he checks, he's gonna get the same story. You hit your head, spent a night in the hospital, there might be brain damage—"

"I don't have brain damage."

"I might've embellished a little around the saloon last night when I went down for a night cap at last call."

She widened her eyes at Eve, and Eve shrugged. "I said it might not be permanent."

"Gee, thanks."

"You're welcome. So, see? Closing the bakery for a few days won't seem strange at all. We can take care of the logistics of selling it once you're settled elsewhere."

Sunny closed her eyes. The thought of selling the bakery was too much. "Mouse and Tabitha depend on their paychecks."

"You depend on your heart to keep beating. Keep your priorities straight."

"I have to make sure no one thinks Jason pushed me, too. And soon."

"We'll deal with all that once you're safe."

Sunny looked around her kitchen, loving it more than ever. Daisies were the theme. There were daisies on the valance above the little window that looked down over the river. There were daisy borders on the walls, and daisy canisters and a set of daisy coffee mugs.

At first that had been pretend, just part of the new persona she'd been building when she'd first come here all dark and wounded and bleak. She'd built a whole being based on what she thought her mother had been like. Her mother would've loved daisies because she was sunshine and light and love and everything good. She wore pastel sundresses and pearls. Sunny had tried to model herself after that imaginary perfection.

She'd enjoyed being Sunny. She'd actually started to believe she really was her.

"Where am I going?" she asked softly as she took her daisy coffee mugs to the bedroom, and tucked them into the small suitcase among her clothes, so they wouldn't break.

"New Mexico," Eve said. I have a small place in this little village outside Taos that's always been my personal backup plan. But now it's yours."

"You have a personal backup plan?"

"You don't do what I do without a backup plan. I figured if I ever got in trouble deep enough that I needed to drop out of sight, I'd head for Plum Creek, New Mexico. You'll love this town. It's as pretty as Big Falls."

"No place is as pretty as Big Falls," Sunny said. "I don't want to leave without my cat, Eve."

"Sunny." Eve put her hands on both her shoulders. "Your cat got out because the door was open, and the door was open because your brother was here looking for you. We're just lucky he didn't find you, or someone to tell him where you were. We'll find the cat. I'll put someone on it, and we'll bring him to you, okay?"

"Her. You'll bring her to me."

"Her, yeah. I knew that. Look, let's get the essentials and get you to safety before it's too late." She frowned as a motor rumbled past. "That same pickup has passed three times."

"Pickup trucks outnumber humans in Big Falls."

"But this one has a hole in the exhaust that makes it sound like shit. We're not taking chances. We can't."

Eve was not being overly cautious. Sunny knew better than anyone what Braxton was capable of. "Are we leaving right now? I told Jimmy I–"

"You told Jimmy you're staying with me tonight over at the Long Branch. I know. So, put most of your stuff in my car, because we're gonna have to leave yours anyway."

"I love that car."

"We'll drive both vehicles over to the Long Branch so everything looks just like we said. And then we slip out in the wee hours, after closing time. Gives us a nice long head start before anyone knows we're even gone."

Sunny's breaths felt like they were shuddering in and out of her. It couldn't be her last night in Big Falls. It couldn't.

Big Falls is magic, Vidalia Brand had told her once. *Local legend is, she chooses her residents. She beams out a siren's call to those who are meant to be here, and once they set foot on her red soil, they stay forever.*

Tears welled up in her eyes.

"Hey," Eve said. "Come on, now, it'll be–"

"I need to grab the cat carrier, in case we find Griz." Sunny hurried out of the room because she didn't want Eve, the strongest woman she knew, to see her cry twice in one day.

CHAPTER 8

*J*ason had a bad feeling gnawing at his gut as he lay in bed trying to sleep. Things weren't right. Sunny wasn't right. She was faking amnesia, plain as day, and just not acting like herself. And how about this Eve person showing up out of nowhere? First time they've seen each other in six years and they're as tight as sisters? It didn't make sense. And someone had busted into her house.

And then there was that tattoo. And that photo. And all the lies.

He rolled to his other side, punching the pillow into submission.

She wouldn't even break character long enough to tell Jimmy the truth, that she'd fallen, that he hadn't put a hand on her. The Sunny he knew would never act this way.

It was all tied up together, he knew it was. And he wanted to know how, because Sunny was in trouble. And he couldn't help her if he didn't know how.

His step-sister was a PI, married to a PI. Hell, so was Angie Wakeland's ex-sister-in-law, Riley. Angie was Sunny's best friend, so that made three professional snoops, practically in the family.

But something told him it wouldn't be right to take that route. If he wanted to know Sunny's secrets, he had to ask Sunny. Not go behind her back digging up a past she apparently wanted to forget.

And she must want to forget it. The Sunny he knew had never shown a sign of hating anyone. She was the least hateful person he'd ever known. She was...she was *Sunny*. Everything about her was the opposite of that hate symbol on her head.

And maybe that was on purpose. Or maybe it was just a lie. But, either way, he wished she'd told him. Dammit, she should've told him.

He wasn't going to sleep.

He got out of bed, scrubbed his hair and walked to the kitchen, trying to decide between warm cocoa or a shot of something alcoholic. Or both.

Yeah. Both.

He poured milk into a pan, and a packet of cocoa mix into a mug. Then he opened his top cupboard for something to spike it with and found bottle of peppermint schnapps that had been there since last Christmas. Perfect.

He was pouring milk over cocoa when he heard something odd near the front door. Not a knock but...something. He set the milk back in the fridge, and then stood still, head cocked, listening. There was only silence. No owls, no coyotes, not even a stiff wind. It was dead quiet tonight. So he stirred the cocoa with one hand and poured the schnapps with the other, and he heard it again. *Scratch, scratch, scratch.*

Picking up his mug, he sipped his way to the front door and opened it.

A cat rubbed around his ankles. He frowned down at it, because it looked a lot like Griz. Then it tipped its face up and purred. Heck, it *was* Griz! "How the heck did you get here?" He tried to remember if he'd heard anyone pull in, but he hadn't. Last thing he'd noticed was a truck going by with an engine that sounded like crap.

He set his drink—which was delicious—on the stand to his right, then crouched slowly. He needed to get the cat inside and close the door quick, so she wouldn't get away, but Griselda had a plan of her own. She shot past him, right into the house.

"Problem solved," he said, closing the door. "I know somebody who's gonna be very happy to see you."

And he was very happy to have an excuse to call Sunny. They needed to talk. Really talk. That wasn't something they'd ever done, and it was high time. Past time.

Her cell phone vibrated.

Sunny had gone to bed with it in her grasp, like a castaway clinging to his last piece of flotsam. Eve would make her get rid of it as soon as they hit the road. It felt like the last bit of her life as Sunny Cantrell. She'd left the rest behind already. Her home, her business, all her things. Even her cat was gone. Soon they'd get rid of her car, too, and all she'd have left would be a few suitcases full of crap. She would keep her phone just as long as she possibly could. It represented so much more than it was.

So, when it vibrated, she woke fast and rolled out of bed, tiptoeing fast across the room, then into the hallway, almost all in one motion.

Downstairs, the juke box played Hank Williams and ice and glasses clinked backup. A low murmur of voices barely reached her. It was only eleven. The Long Branch closed at two.

She answered the phone with a whispered "Hello?"

"Hey."

It was Jason! Her heart lurched hard. "H-hey."

"Sorry to call so late, but I have a visitor here."

Her blood went cold. Her brother had found him. "Ohmy-God, Jason are you all right?"

"Fine. I'm fine. Why would you–Sunny, are *you* all right?"

"No. I'm really not."

"That's the first honest thing you've said to me since you hit your head."

She said nothing. She didn't know what to say. He was in danger. He'd said someone was there. "Who is your visitor, Jason?"

"Griselda."

It took a beat to register. "Griselda's there?"

"Don't ask me how or why. But I found her scratching at my door. And get this. She rubbed around my ankles, then walked in like she owned the place."

Sunny went almost limp with relief. Griselda was his visitor. Not her brother or one of his slathering followers. "Thank God." She said it on a sigh. "Is she okay?"

"Looks fine to me. She's had a can of tuna, a sip of the finest tap water, and now she's grooming herself on the back of my sofa."

"I'll come get her."

"It's late. I'll bring her to you in the morning."

But in the morning, I'll be gone.

"I um. I need her now. I don't…I can't explain, I just really need my cat."

"I can bring–"

"I'm coming over. I'll see you soon."

She disconnected and went back into the room. Eve was sitting up in bed, waiting for her. "Jason?" she asked.

Sunny nodded. "He found Griz. I'm going over to get her. And…to say goodbye."

"You can't tell him we're leaving."

"I know."

"You can't tell him anything, Sunny."

74

"I know, Eve. This isn't my first rodeo. This will be the last time I'll..." Her throat tightened, and she had to force a swallow to go on. "The last time I'll ever see him."

"Oh, *hell* no." Eve slapped the covers on either side of her.

"What?"

"You're in love, that's what." She flipped back her blankets and got up. "Damn, Sunny, you *can't* be in love."

"I'm not in love. I've taken great pains not to fall in love."

"Oh, you have." Deadpan. Eve started putting on the clothes she'd left out last night. Everything else was packed and they'd both showered before sleeping. The only things not packed were the clothes and shoes they'd wear to leave, and their tooth-brushes.

"Yes, I have."

"Then why are there little red hearts instead of pupils in your eyes? You knew better." Eve finished buttoning her shirt and pulled on her jeans.

"Look," Sunny said. "I'll be back in a few hours. And I'll have my cat and we can go, just like you planned. Okay?"

"Not okay. It's not safe. I have to go with you."

"Absolutely not."

"I'll wait in the car."

"And that's not gonna look suspicious? You lurking in the driveway like some kind of Aunt Lydia?"

"I'll park down the road out of sight. But within shouting distance. It's that or nothing."

"I might...be a while."

Eve closed her eyes and strung six cuss words together in a creative and unique manner. Then she said. "Fine. I'll wait. Now get dressed, and let's get this show on the road."

~

Jason watched Sunny's car pull into his driveway. Another vehicle passed, headlights briefly spilling on her as she got out of the car and came toward his front door. He scooped up the cat and opened it before she even knocked.

Her eyes met his, and there was this long, awkward thing hanging between them. Her lies, maybe, or his own unasked questions.

Then she looked at the cat, who was not twisting or scratching or even growling in his arms.

"Aw, there she is," she said softly. "Hey, Griz. And look at you holding her. She's not even-" She bit off the rest.

Scratching you, he thought. That's what she was going to say. *She's not even scratching you.* But that would imply she remembered how Griz would just casually walk up and take a swipe at him for kicks. Which, she didn't. Right? Because amnesia.

"I know," he said instead of calling her on it. Not yet. It wasn't time. She was here. She'd come to him. He'd been praying she would, even knowing about her lies. "We've been working on it for a couple of hours, and I finally found a scratch-proof hold." He turned as he said it, so she could see.

Griz gave her an icy glance, then closed her eyes.

"I think she just cussed me out in Feline." She reached for the cat. "Thank you."

"You're welcome." Jason didn't let Griz go, and instead, side-stepped and opened the door wider. "Can you...come in for a minute?" He looked deep into her eyes, trying to see the truth. What was going on? Why was she pretending to have lost her memory?

Her eyes flicked toward the road and back again.

"Only for a minute." She stepped inside.

He closed the door and let Griz leap out of his arms. She trotted into the living room jumped onto the sofa, then started kneading it into proper napping consistency.

He looked at Sunny. She looked at him. He said, "I miss you, Sunny. I miss us."

"Me, too."

"Then you *do* remember."

She stepped a little closer, tipped her head just slightly to one side, her chin tilting up a little, her lips parting, her invitation clear. He kissed her softly, and then, when her arms twisted around his neck, not as softly. She tasted like he remembered. She wasn't different. He'd know if she was someone else.

When he stopped and lifted his head, he stared into her big blue eyes, looking for her secrets. "I have so many questions."

"I know. I know you do. Can you let 'em go, Jason? Just for now?" She pressed herself closer.

"Uh-huh," he said. And then he kissed her again, and still kissing her, pulled her up off her feet. She wrapped her legs around his waist, arms tighter around his neck and he carried her that way, into his bedroom.

They fell on the bed, undressed each other, explored each other, worshipped each other like they never had before. Every touch was more intense, every taste more exciting. There was something desperate about it, and the pinnacle was shattering.

They held each other for a long time, her head on his chest, her body all twisted up with his. They didn't move or speak, waiting for their pieces to reassemble.

He lay there, with her hair spread over his chest, and thought it had been different than ever before. *She* was different. Something in her had shifted, somehow.

Sunny lay in Jason's arms, the safest place in the whole world. Maybe the only safe place in the world for her. She nodded off and dreamed of the day she'd met Dave. She'd been sitting on the bench at her first college softball game, backup pitcher to

Gigi Hannaford. Gigi was amazing, had a stellar record and another year to go.

Mary had been so proud when the college coach had praised her pitching skills. She'd seen her high school tapes, she said. She knew a champ in the making. She could spot 'em, she'd said. And then she'd given her a uniform, a practice schedule, and a seat on the bench.

That's where she'd been when Dave had walked right into the dugout, like he had a right to be there, and said, "Hey, Coach, you care if I talk to your girl, Mary, for a minute?"

Coach nodded. "Hustle up, Hayes." Then to him, "Five minutes."

"Got it."

She thought, for a second, of what her father might think if he saw this, a middle-aged Latina giving her permission to leave the dugout with a young black man. She'd pondered on what her father might think about a lot of things since coming to college. Her roommate was Mexican. Her advisor, Jewish. Her favorite professor, Japanese. There were all kinds of people on this campus, and none of them seemed like what her father said they were. No one seemed to be conspiring to take over the country or replace "the white man." None of them seemed any different from her. Her father's way of thinking was wrong. It was just plain wrong. She'd come fully awake to that within her first few weeks on campus. Nothing was the way he said it was. Nothing. And no one.

"You there, Hayes?"

She blinked, and realized Dave had been talking to her. And that he was movie star good looking. "I'm sorry," she said. "I was thinking."

"You know who I am?" he asked. He'd walked her around behind the dugout. It was pretty private there.

"You're Dave Barron. You pitch for the baseball team."

"That's right."

"I've seen your games, when we're not playing elsewhere at the same time. You're good."

"Thank you. Listen, I came over her because uh...well, let's be frank. You look a little morose sitting there on the bench."

"Yeah. I thought I'd be in the game."

"You will be. You're better than her, you know."

"Who? Gigi?"

He nodded. "I've seen you at practice a few times. I know pitchers, and you're a pitcher. You've just gotta bide your time and wait your turn. This is her dream, too, and she got here first. So, you just wait it out, because your turn's next, and the whole time you're out there killing it, there's gonna be a freshman on the bench, wishing it was her turn."

She lifted her brows. "Where did you get all this old-man wisdom?"

"It's what my coach told me when he saw *me* sitting the bench, looking morose my first year on the team. And then he told me to put a smile on my face if it killed me or I wouldn't last long enough to get my turn."

That startled her.

"It looks bad if the backup's over here pouting. And it's bad for team morale, and it's probably getting under Gigi's helmet to boot. You should be cheering for her louder than anybody. Louder than her own family when they come. Her success is the team's success, and the team's success is your success."

She nodded slowly. "That's really deep."

"That part's original," he said with a proud tip of his head. "So...you get it?"

"I get it. I'm being an asshole."

"There you go."

They both laughed. She noticed his eyes, brown and kind and knowing. He seemed to notice her noticing. "You're pretty, Hayes. And funny, too. You, um...you want to have coffee sometime?"

Her brows went up like they had springs on them. "You and me?"

"Be a whole new experience for you, huh? But then again, that's what college is for."

"Hayes, time's up!" Coach called.

She started to head back, then turned around. "Coffee sounds good. How about tomorrow? I've got no classes after two."

"Meet you at The Bean at two thirty then."

She smiled a smile that felt like it started at her toes and worked its way up. He smiled back. And she thought, *it's a good thing Dad and Brax never come to my games.* And it was the first time she'd ever thought it.

And then she hustled back to the dugout. But she didn't sit on the bench. she went right up to the grill and starting clapping and shouting, "Go, Hannaford! You got this!"

Gigi threw a strike. Mary whistled and clapped and shouted some more.

She saw Gigi pause before winding up and glance her way, and send her a smile. She felt good inside. And she liked that feeling.

Jason let Sunny sleep. She probably needed it. He had his head propped up so he could look at her, all peaceful and relaxed across him. She was so damn pretty. She had a cute little nose, short and a little bit wide, a fairy's nose. That, and the all-but-invisible spray of freckles across her cheekbones had probably not changed since she'd been a little girl.

She'd scooped her hair all over to one side to cover her stitches and that horror on her scalp. What was she doing with a swastika tattoo? Lying to him, faking amnesia? Coming over here in the middle of the night and making love to him like never before? Like it was their last time or something.

She must've felt his eyes on her, because she blinked hers open, smiled up at him, and said, "I dozed off."

"Only for a few minutes." The clock said 12:20.

She trailed a hand over his chest, then pushed herself up, turned, and started gathering up her clothes on the way to his bathroom. From there, she called, "I have to go. I hate to, but I have to."

He got up and dressed too, and when she came back out, he said, "Before you do, there's something I want to show you."

She came out, met him halfway. "Sounds mysterious."

"It's ...something I've been keeping to myself. This way." He took her across the living room to the door that led to the attached workshop and reached for the doorknob.

"If you've got some *Fifty Shades* kind of thing going on in there, I don't think–"

"*Fifty Shades*, huh?" He shook his head at her. "*That* you remember?" He opened the door, turned on the light, and watched her face as she followed him in. He'd never taken her into his workshop before. He'd never taken anyone in there. He'd deemed it off limits to his family. He'd told Sunny once that it was his private space, and she'd never asked again. He got why now. She understood secrets. She had plenty of her own.

He watched her as she stepped through and looked around.

She saw the swords first. Probably because of the way they caught the light and reflected it. There was barely room to hang one more on the walls.

He watched her eyes take them in. She breathed an appreciative "Wow." And then, "So you collect swords? That's your private thing?"

"I *make* swords"

And that's when she swung her head around and her big

eyes met his. "You *made* these? Jason, you *made these*? All of them?"

"Yeah."

She walked away from him, up to the nearest wall, and then moved slowly, tipping her head up to examine every piece. "What about the um…sword holders? Eagle talons, dragon's claws, every sort of animal paw, hoof and claw. Did you make those, too?"

"Most of 'em. It's a…a hobby. But I'm kind of passionate about it."

"This is no hobby. It's art. You're an *artist*, Jason." Then she said, "That's why you bought this place. It used to be a smithy's shop, didn't it?"

She might remember that bit of local history, or she might know just from looking around. It was obvious if you paid attention. "Right. The original forge is still here." He nodded at it. It was in the center of the room, a giant iron beast. Its chimney shot straight up through the roof. Beside it stood its modern counterpart. "I use it quite a lot."

"I am…absolutely…just…this is incredible." She was still looking around the place, and then at him, and then around the walls again. "How could you not tell me this?"

He could have asked how she knew he'd never told her, if she had no memory. But she really wasn't pretending very hard at that lie anymore.

"It's just something I've always kept to myself," he said.

"But why?" She tipped her head to one side, like there were glyphs she was trying to translate appearing on his face. "This is kind of a big deal. It's like…it's who you are."

"I don't know. Why does anyone keep their true self hidden?" He watched her face, tried to hold onto her eyes, but she wouldn't let him. She turned away so he couldn't.

"I've been asking myself why for a while now," he went on. "Maybe I care too much about what others might think. That it's a silly way to spend time and money. That I've got more money than brains. I don't know. But maybe keeping it to myself is mostly because it's my own. All my paying work has been helping my dad with the businesses he created. Even the Long Branch was his project, and now Joey's really making it his own. But even before I sold my share, it never felt like mine. This...this is mine."

"It's not silly. These blades are worth a fortune all by themselves. My God, look at them all." She shook her head, moving through the shop. "Is this all of them?"

"Not all, no. I give a lot away. I have ten in the truck right now, packed up to travel. I'm donating them to a charity auction."

"Of course you are."

She ran her hand over the handle of his favorite Katana, the one with the dragon's head. Then she took a deep breath, and turned to face him again. She'd walked several steps away, and around to the rear of the room. The mechanical hammer stood between them, but she met his eyes around it, and asked quite sincerely, "Why are you sharing this with me now?"

He shrugged. "Because I want you to share your true self with me. And because I had no right to ask that when I hadn't done the same. But I'm aware you've been lying to me, Sunny. I saw the photo, the one behind your mother's. The one of your family, and your baby brother–".

"Don't."

"This conversation has to happen. Do you know I was formally questioned by the police?"

"By your brother-in-law, you mean."

"Bernie Jennings thinks I pushed you. He thinks I *pushed you*, Sunny, and his wife Betty Lou is the biggest gossip in town. And you're here playing whatever you're playing instead of telling the truth about what happened."

"I'm sorry!" She covered her face with her hands, in shame or remorse or self-defense. He was damned if he knew which. "I'm sorry, I'm sorry, I'm sorry."

He stopped talking. She looked like she might break if he kept talking. "Just tell me why. That's all I want, just tell me why."

She lowered her hands slowly, took a long time wiping the tears away. "When I can, I will." Then she looked to his right, desperate, he thought, for a different subject. "What's that curved one there?" She nodded at the workbench, where an unfinished project lay.

It took a long beat to answer. He thought about refusing to let her change the subject, but her tears were real. He knew by looking at her that she was at the ragged edge of her endurance. She hadn't looked this bad since that Christmas a few years back, when her friend Angie's husband was killed in action.

"Mongolian throwing sword," he said. He picked it up, balanced it on two upturned fingers. "I need to do a little more grinding on it."

"Oh. Do you actually know how to throw it?"

"Yeah. I do Kendo. It's a martial art thing with swords, and..." He let his words trail off. "Please say something, Sunny. Tell me something, for everything we've been to each other, just tell me something."

"Jason, I–"

The outside door crashed open and a man stood there pointing a gun at them. Jason's reflexes kicked in; he turned and threw the knife. It cartwheeled beautifully, and then its blade embedded itself deep in the guy's chest. The gun went off as the shooter went down. Jason looked to see if Sunny was okay, but she wasn't there.

CHAPTER 9

Sunny had never seen anything like it. Jason flexed his hand, the one balancing the blade, and it jumped up a little, then he snatched it from the air and moved like a dancer, one foot forward, his body twisting, his arm pivoting at the shoulder, then elbow. The blade whirled and hit its mark. The intruder's gun went off as he fell down.

She saw it all in slowed-down time, as she ducked behind a big machine, wrapping her arms around her knees and burying her face there. Her whole body was shaking. She knew that guy. He was Braxton's best friend, Landry Mason. My God, Brax had found her.

Eve sprang through the same doorway, jumping the fallen man with a gun in her hands. She looking around, and then down at him before she holstered her weapon. "Where's Sunny?"

At the sound of Eve's voice, Sunny rose from her crouch. She was shaking so bad she could hardly walk, but she made it into Jason's arms and they closed around her like they always did.

"Are you okay?" he asked, holding her, rocking her. Like he cared. Like she hadn't ruined everything with him.

She nodded against his chest. Her cheek pressed there, and she was facing Eve, who mouthed GO NOW.

Sunny sniffled. "Call Chief Jimmy," she said. "I'm okay."

"My phone's inside."

"I'm okay. Go on, you have to let him know. Get him out here. It was self-defense. I saw it. I'll back you up." She wasn't going to, though. She was going to leave again. God, she hated herself, felt like garbage for not insisting to Jimmy that he hadn't pushed her. But it was only until he was safe—only until she got herself and her sibling far away from him, so he would be safe. Then she'd tell everyone the truth, somehow. She'd find a way.

"We'll all go in." Jason took her arm gently and tugged her inside, like he didn't trust her out of his sight. It wasn't that. He was protecting her. He'd get killed protecting her. Griz pounced on her shin as soon as she stepped inside. She'd been neglected and she was not happy about it.

Sunny picked her up, hugged her and kissed her fur. Then she walked up to Jason, stood on tiptoe, and kissed him hard. "I have to go and you have to let me."

He shook his head, but didn't reach for her as she turned around, grabbed Eve's hand and ran.

She held Griz in one arm as she jumped over the body of Landry Mason, her brother's best friend, and broke into a run. If Landry was here, then so was Brax. He was like a wolf with a pack of simpering dogs. He never went anywhere without his "boys."

And Jason had just killed one of them.

"Brax will kill him," Sunny said, not breaking stride.

"I think your guy can handle himself. What's with the medieval armory anyway?"

"He made them. I never even knew."

Sunny felt as if there were gun sites on her back as they raced through the brush beside Jason's house into a tree lot, and out the other side to the road, and Eve's car.

"My purse and my phone are still in my car!" Sunny cried, having only just realized it.

"We'd have had to toss those anyway." Eve opened the passenger door and shoved Sunny in, cat and all, then slammed it on her and shot around to her own side.

Griz clawed free of Sunny's arms and dove into the back seat. She let the cat go as they sped away, leaving a trail of dust behind them like a comet's tail.

A trail of dust—and her life. And every link she'd had to it. And Jason. Jason, just when things had turned...bigger. Deeper. Better.

Jason ran outside, cell phone in hand.

"Hey, Jason," his sort of brother-in-law said, sounding cheerful. "How's—"

"I just killed a man, Jimmy. Out at my place. Get out here fast." He was at the doorway, looking to see which way they'd gone. "Sunny?" And then more urgently. "Sunny!"

A car spit gravel, its engine growling from someplace nearby. Then he heard something else. A groan.

"Jason? What's going on?" Jimmy asked. "Is Sunny all right?"

"Sunny took off," Jason said, bending down near the intruder's body. "She left her car. Must've gone with Eve." He laid his hand on the guy's chest, to the left of the blade. "Also, the intruder ain't dead. But he's got a Mongolian throwing sword in his chest."

"A Mongolian what?"

"I gotta put the phone down and try to stop the bleeding." He did, and then took off his outer shirt, wadded it up and pressed it around the spot where the blade was stuck into the intruder's chest. Bright red blood bubbled all around the honed steel. He'd have far rather been chasing after Sunny, but he couldn't just let the guy bleed out on his floor.

"Hey, asshat. Wake up." He had unruly hair in no particular style, and lots of ink. Jason had nothing against tattoos. They were art. Well, they were supposed to be art. His were mostly trash.

"Come on, I have questions. Unless you want me to just let you die." He was feeling kind of relieved that he hadn't killed the guy, and he was going to do whatever he could to keep him alive, but the gunman didn't have to know that.

He opened his eyes. They slanted downward, then widened. "Who the hell does that?"

"Me, when someone kicks in my door and points a gun at me."

"Not at you. Her. Mary."

"Who the hell's Mary?" But he already knew the thug was talking about Sunny.

"Her car's in your driveway." He sucked air through his teeth. "Her cat was in your... Get that thing outta my chest."

"I'm no MD, but I'm afraid that might kill you."

"I can't feel my legs."

"I'm sorry for you. Maybe rethink your life choices. If you live, I mean."

He winced in pain. Jason said, "Help's on the way. Listen. Hear the sirens?"

"No."

"I do. They'll be here in a minute. Maybe less. What do you have against her? Mary?"

He whispered too softly for Jason to hear, so Jason leaned

closer, and the guy said, almost full voice, "None of your fucking business."

Jimmy's SUVs skidded to a stop on the lawn and he came running, knelt beside the fallen man, and just gaped, first at the blade and then at Jason, and then at the workshop behind Jason. Yeah, too many surprises all at once, Jason figured. He shook himself, spotted the gun four feet away, and quickly went to grab it with a plastic bag. The ambulance came barreling in right behind him, and then medics were shoving Jason aside to take over. There were more cops arriving, lighting up the night like a laser show, and a chopper landed out back. His brothers' pickups were only seconds behind the rest.

Yeah, small town. Tight family. There were no secrets here. He'd managed to keep a small one, and it looked like Sunny had kept a great big giant sized one, a dangerous one.

Jimmy said, "I need to hear it from the beginning."

"Yeah," Jason said. "I figured you would."

Eve drove like a maniac, took the highway going west, and then skidded into the parking area of an out-of-business motel. The pavement was cracked and busted, even heaving in some spots, and there was only one other car. She pulled right up beside it, braked to a sharp stop, and popped her trunk.

"Grab everything from this car and throw it into that one," she ordered. "Go! Fast, in case anyone followed."

Sunny grabbed Griz from the back seat, already regretting that his carrier was still in her own car at Jason's place. She held Griselda carefully and ran to the other car. There was a cat carrier in its back seat. For a second she just blinked.

Eve came running behind her with a backpack and two suitcases. "Will you get the lead out?"

"There's a cat carrier."

"There are some generic essentials, too. I like to be prepared." Eve slammed the trunk and grabbed her shoulders. "We have to go. Get in the car."

Sunny got into the back seat, so she could put Griz in the carrier. The irritated cat didn't like it, but went in without a fight. Eve had run back to the other car again, and Sunny got out to help.

"Get the stuff from the console!" Eve told her. "Hurry!"

Nodding, Sunny leaned in, opened the console between the bucket seats. The only thing inside was a silver handgun in a brown leather holster. She grabbed the gun, backed out, closed the car door, ran to the second car and got into the passenger side. This car had a console, too, so she dropped the gun into it. Eve dove behind the wheel and they were on the highway again before a single other vehicle had passed.

Then Eve adjusted the rearview mirror, and watched it while she tapped a button on her keyring. Behind them, Eve's gorgeous little car exploded like something out of an action movie, and Sunny thought her heart was going to pop right out of her chest it startled her so much.

"Holy God, Eve!"

"Distraction," she said. "Too many people are looking for us. We leave the car just sitting there, it's an easy bet we switched vehicles. This way, they don't know anything for sure.

"But Jason might think—"

"You've gotta let that go, Sunny."

"I will *not* let it go. Jason is in danger because of me. Suspected of hurting me, and maybe murder now, too because the only witnesses are running for their lives. And now you want me to let him think I burned alive in that car?"

"He's perfectly safe. By now he's surrounded by cops and relatives and cops who are also relatives."

"Who don't know what they're dealing with. I want him

protected, and I want you to do it now, or I swear to God I'll jump out of this car, Eve. You know I'll do it."

Eve sighed and tapped a button on the car's in-dash system. Her phone was already connected to it. She wasn't kidding about being prepared. Her call went out. A man answered. "Santorini."

"It's DuVall."

"We're secure, go ahead."

"Jason McIntyre of Big Falls just killed Landry Mason in self-defense. He'll need protection."

"Mason's still alive," the guy on the other end said. Sunny's heart tripped over itself as the stranger she presumed was an FBI contact went on. "They airlifted him to a trauma unit. And we've got a guy on McIntyre. We might bring in the local PD–"

"I wouldn't. The chief is McIntyre's brother in law, and it's a tight family. They don't keep things quiet in Big Falls."

"All right. You safe?"

"Not yet."

"Need help?"

"Not yet." She tapped the cutoff. "That's Roberto Santorini, my boss. He's always Uncle Bob on every cell phone I have. If you get into trouble and I'm out of commission, that's who to call."

She shifted in her seat. "I can't let Jason worry I'm dead in that car, Eve. Not Kiley or Angie, either. Not even for a little while. It's too cruel. I won't do it."

Eve sighed. "I'll take it under advisement."

"You'll take it under–no. I'll get out and walk back to Big Falls."

"They won't find the car for eighteen to twenty-four hours. We have time for me to mull on this. So let me mull, Sunny. Or maybe I should start calling you Jill?"

"Huh?"

"You're Jillian Mueller, a kindergarten teacher from Ohio.

All your papers are being sent to a PO Box in New Mexico. Credit cards, driver's license, social, fresh new birth certificate, teaching credentials, the whole nine. And a thumb drive with your new backstory."

Sunny let her head drop back against the seat. "God, I don't want to do this again."

"You'd rather let your brother kill you?"

Why do those have to be the only two choices? Stay and risk my life and Jason's life, or run and leave it all behind?"

"Because they are." Eve had these round, expressive eyes that didn't match the hardass behind them. "They are, Sunny. They're the *only* two choices. You run or you die. Braxton is a crazy son of a bitch, but he's served his time. He's out. And he's smart enough to send his mongrels to do his dirty work for him. We've got nothing on him.

Sunny closed her eyes and let the tears fall. She'd lost everything. Again.

Eve was quiet for a moment. She had the good sense to let her grieve in private, and Sunny appreciated it. She *was* grieving. She was grieving the death of Sunny Cantrell, and Sunny's Place, the little bakery with the pink and white striped awning that stood out from all the other awnings on all the other businesses on Main Street. Almost like she was trying to tell them, right from the start, *I'm not one of you. I'm only pretending to be. But underneath, this is all a lie. I'm a lie.*

"It was nice, the life you made. You should be proud of that," Eve said after a while. "That bakery, and the friendships. And him."

She sniffled, saying nothing.

"You never knew he was a swordsmith, huh?"

"He never told me. Not until today. And the way he moved, the way he threw that blade, that was something, too. Some kind of martial arts thing."

"And you never knew he was into that, either?"

She shook her head.

"Huh."

Sunny twisted in her seat to look at Eve. They'd become friends, back in the old days. Eve had saved her life. And given her a new one. And now she was doing it again.

Sunny loved Eve DuVall. She was smart, tough, ripped, and kind. And she was honest right to her core. "What does that mean?"

"What does what mean?"

"That *huh*. It meant something, I can tell."

Eve shrugged. "Just...you're pretty busted up over leaving a guy you really never knew."

"He never really knew me, either."

"He knew Sunny Cantrell, and that's who you were in Big Falls. You created this happy, bright, successful woman everybody loved. And you know, that's part of who you are, way down deep. It has to be, she came from you."

"Maybe," she said. "She's me if my past never happened. She's me on vacation from me. And now I have to create someone else. Someone new."

"You could be a redhead this time. That's a plus."

Sunny closed her eyes. "I hate this. I hate it."

"I hate it for you," Eve said, and she meant it.

Jason's little house was crowded with family within an hour. Jimmy had finished with his questions, but told him to keep the workshop locked and not set foot inside until he gave him the okay. He was pretty sure Jimmy believed him. But that wouldn't matter much if the evidence said otherwise. He had no eye witnesses, except the victim, if he pulled through. But that guy wasn't gonna tell the truth.

Kiley was there, hanging close to him, trying to pry information out of him in the most gentle, subtle, transparent ways. Angie stayed nearby, too, mothering him a little bit. Angie's kid sister was watching all the kids, including her own toddler. Besides the two of them, most of the people crowded into his little house were family. His father was pacing and looking worried, and stepmom Vidalia was trying to comfort and reassure everyone. Mouse and Tabitha, had just arrived, and like the rest, made a beeline for him to start asking questions he couldn't answer.

Jason held up a hand and cut loose a whistle. Everyone went quiet and turned to look his way. Jack Kellogg came in about then, and wandered to the very back of the crowd to stand near the kitchen.

Jason said, "I'm gonna fill you all in at once, and then I need to get out looking for Sunny. Sunny was here with me when a stranger kicked in the door of my workshop and leveled a gun at us. I had a throwing knife in my hand and I reacted. He's still alive, in the ICU. Jimmy's looking into who he is and what he was after."

Kiley said, "Is this the same guy who broke into Sunny's place last night?"

"We don't know."

"Well, where's Sunny now?" Angie asked.

"We don't know that, either. She took off with her friend Eve. She was probably pretty shaken up after what happened. She saw the whole thing. We thought I'd killed the guy, at first."

"Who the heck is Eve? I've never heard her mention anyone named Eve," Angie said. "Have you, Kiley?"

"Not once. And she tells me everything."

Way behind everyone, Jack Kellogg shook his head left and right.

"Is she in danger, Jason?" Kiley asked.

"No," he said. And this time, Jack nodded. No one could see him but Jason, who was facing him. Everyone between them

94

was focused solely on Jason. He'd talk to Jack later. For now, he continued trying to calm the gang. "I don't think she's in danger. Even if this guy *was* targeting her and not me, he's no threat now. Frankly, I think he was just some nutcase. I think it was random."

Jack closed his eyes and silently mouthed *nope.*

"Jason, what were you doing with a throwing knife?" That was Joey. "Where did you even get one, much less learn how to use it?"

His pretty wife Emily was close beside him. Little Matilda wasn't with them, and Jason was glad of that. For some reason, he still felt uneasy, like this wasn't the end of the trouble that had come to Big Falls. Like maybe it was only the beginning.

"The blade's a long story best saved for another time."

"Digest version?" his brother Rob asked.

He hesitated, but the fastest way to get them all out of here so he could go hunt for Sunny was to give them what they wanted. "I make swords and knives and things out in the workshop—which you can't see right now because it's a crime scene. So don't ask."

"You make swords?" his father asked. "You...*make* swords?"

"And knives. That's why I bought this place, for the old forge and the history."

Vidalia put a hand on his shoulder and said, "That's amazing, Jason."

"Now, if there's nothing else, folks, I just really want to—"

Kiley said, "We all want to look for her, too. Maybe we can coordinate things from here and—"

"No." He said it too fast and too loud. Everyone reacted with surprise, followed by more questions, until he said, "Look, this guy, whoever he was, and whatever he wanted, came here. *Here* to my home. And we still don't know what this was about. He's probably a lone maniac, but on the off chance he's not, I don't want any of you in the line of fire. I want you all to go home. Be safe. Keep your kids safe. And the minute I know of any way for any of you to help Sunny, believe me, I'll tell you. Okay?"

They just looked at him, like his words were not quite penetrating.

Vidalia came to stand beside him, and putting one hand on his upper arm, she said, "Let's all gather at the Corral. We can continue this discussion there. There's more room anyway."

They responded to that, everyone moving around to obey the matriarch. She patted Jason's arm and said, "They feel helpless. We have to give them something to do, even if it's just busy work. I'll handle 'em. You do what you need to. But Jason, if it's not safe here, then you'd best not be staying here, either." She leaned up and kissed his cheek. "Sunny's a good woman. I know a good woman when I see one. Raised five myself. I'm never wrong. She's a good one. You find her and keep her safe, you hear? And once you do get her back here, you'd best put a ring on her finger before you find yourself left behind like a heathen at The Rapture."

He saw his father look at his brothers and give a nod. Vidalia gathered up Emily and Kiley. Angie Wakeland came to say goodbye, and slipped a business card into his hand. "Riley's agency, in case you need her. She can find anybody."

"Thanks." He gave her a hug, and when she left, he looked at the card in his palm. Everett Investigations. Huh. Riley had taken back her maiden name. He didn't know why that surprised him, but it did. He'd always figured her and Angie's big brother Adam would reconcile, sooner or later. They'd seemed meant to be.

Maybe nothing was ever meant to be. Maybe things were meant for the moment. He and Sunny used to be good. Solid. Now he didn't know who Sunny was. And he wondered if he ever had.

That's bullshit. I know her. I know her essence. I know her heart. Whatever came before, I can't forget the girl I know.

He pocketed the card, just in case.

The rest of the crowd cleared out behind them. But Joey and Rob remained.

"You don't really think we're gonna let you deal with this on your own, do you?" Rob asked. "Besides, I want to get a look at those swords."

Joey grinned. "I've already seen 'em. Sneaked in there one night when you stayed over at Sunny's."

"Then why did you ask where I got the throwing sword," Jason asked.

"So you'd have to admit it."

"You little shit," Rob said. "You never told me."

"Hey, it wasn't my secret to tell. But this one, now," he shifted his focus to Jason. "This one's different. So how about you tell us what you didn't tell everyone else so we can get busy finding Sunny?"

Jason didn't want to tell his brothers anything that would change how they thought of Sunny. He hadn't given up bringing her into the family just yet, although it wasn't looking good. His first job was to make sure she was okay, and protecting her included keeping her secrets. "When there's something to tell you, I'll tell you."

He looked around for Jack to avoid his brothers' probing. He'd intended to grab him for a minute and make him explain himself. But Rob's con-man father-in-law had slipped away with the crowd.

CHAPTER 10

*E*ve decided to drive in a pretzel knot, so it would never be clear where they were heading. Twice, she'd switched cars, and she used a different name and driver's license each time. She was good at her job. All day they played this game, grabbing takeout, then starting off in a new direction with a new car.

There was a rhyme and a reason to the route she chose. Eve didn't think Sunny knew that, but there was. She had to be sure they'd lost their pursuers before she took Sunny to her haven.

Eventually from somewhere in northeastern Oklahoma, she changed course again. They were heading southwest to cut across Texas and into New Mexico.

They'd spent all day driving in loops and curlicues. But Eve knew when it was safe to stop and rest. She used a pre-paid credit card, first to get takeout from a fast-food drive-thru that was open all night, and then for a room. The place was so far off the beaten path, it gave her *Bates Motel* flashbacks. Even creepier in the dead of night.

"Maybe I should've gone with that Red Roof Inn thirty miles back."

Sunny said, "No, this is better. Less busy."

Eve handed Sunny the key, then told herself she should probably start thinking of her as Jillian. Not yet though. Sunny wasn't committed to this yet. She was still too attached to her life and the boyfriend she apparently didn't know too well, and the best friends she'd mentioned a half dozen times since they'd hit the road. Kiley and Angie. Angie and Kiley. Blah blah blah. Eve knew who they were. She'd kept tabs. Angie Wakeland was a war hero's widow. Two kids, a boy and a girl, and had a PI ex-sister-in-law. Kiley, she now knew, was the daughter of the slickest confidence man ever, Jack Kellogg.

For someone with big secrets, Sunny hadn't been too choosey about her friends.

"I'll get the bags," Eve said. "You should get inside, out of sight."

"It's the middle of the night and no one here knows me. God, I don't even know where we are."

"Good. Let's hope your brother doesn't, either."

Sunny juggled the takeout bags, the cat carrier and the room key. She wore bicycle length denim capris, a floral on white top and a button-down sweater, pale blue.

Eve thought she understood now. She had full on *become* Sunny Cantrell, hadn't she?

The transformation had started before the new identity, though, when she'd gone off to college, and her name had still been Mary. Eve knew as much about that time as if she'd been her roomie. Big mistake on Harrison Hayes's part, letting his little girl go to college. Letting her be exposed to other ways of thinking, other ways of being. Letting her see that not everyone hated. She'd made friends with people of other races, other religions, from other countries, cultures and political parties. She'd fallen in love with all of them and with one of them, in particular. Dave Barron.

And that had been his death sentence.

Eve took her time behind the open trunk, transferring just enough for an overnight stay from her bulging duffel bag into the two smaller packs she'd brought along, one for each of them. As soon as Sunny was inside with the door closed, Eve pulled out her phone, scrolled to the pic of that smiling devil Jack Kellogg, and tapped CALL. She didn't trust him as far as she could throw him, but she needed his help.

He answered on the fourth ring, with a groggy, "Whaswrong?"

"Wake up, Jack. It's Eve."

She heard what she assumed was the rustle of bedding, it being after midnight. He cleared his throat. "Eve?"

"Yeah."

"Sunny with you? Kiley's losing her shit over here."

"Yeah. You can tell Kiley she's fine, but that's all, Jack. I don't want anyone in town to know the truth about Sunny's past."

"I can do that–"

"Thanks."

"–if you tell me why not."

"What do you mean, why not?"

"You got her out of town so fast you left the place spinning. I'm the only one who knows she's not coming back and that she's not even Sunny anymore. So what difference does it make if people find out she's really the daughter of that racist shithead Harry Hayes?"

She took a breath, schooled her voice calm. He might just be fishing. "What makes you think that?"

"I met Harry in prison. He had photos of his kids. I had photos of mine. I knew who Sunny was the first time I set eyes on her in Big Falls."

"And you never told anyone."

"Kiley loves her, what'm'I gonna do? It'll break my girl's heart when Sunny doesn't come back. But knowing why might help. So why the secrecy? Does it still really matter?"

Eve tucked the phone between her ear and shoulder and rooted through one of Sunny's bags. "I don't know if she's done there, yet."

"You don't say."

"I can't force her. She's got free will and she's not letting go easy."

"Huh. What do you know about that? Maybe what they say about this little town isn't grade-A bullshit after all."

"And what do they say about that little town?"

"Unimportant. I'm glad you called, Eve. Braxton's here in Big Falls. I saw him skulking around at the Long Branch earlier. Met that asshole in prison, too, short time he spent there. You gotta love a system where a cold-blooded killer does less time than a gentleman grifter."

"You're no gentleman, Jack."

"Gentleman Jack. I like that. So why are you calling? Seeing me again get all those old flames flickering?"

"You wish. I need someone who knows Big Falls and her residents well enough to keep me informed on what's up with the locals, and more importantly, with Braxton Hayes."

"You want me to be your CI? Again, Eve?" Then his voice turned soft and deeper. "As I recall, I enjoyed that a lot, last time."

"That's not gonna happen again."

He gave an exaggerated sigh. "I'll help you out for the right price. I've got no sentence to reduce this time."

"I could end your parole."

"That and ten grand might buy my assistance."

"I can get *one*."

"Five."

"Two."

"Three," he said.

She smiled, because she could've given him five. "Twenty-five hundred. That's all I can do for you."

"Deal, cheapskate. And as your new confidential informant, I'll tell you there were dozens of do-gooders out beating the bushes in search of your girl all day long, including my daughters. They'd better not get hurt."

"Brax will leave town as soon as he realizes Sunny's skipped," she said.

"You sure?"

"Pretty sure, yeah."

"Is this number gonna stay good?"

"It's a burner," she told him. "I'll dump it when I hang up, get another tomorrow. Better if you wait for me to call you."

"Sure," Jack said.

"I torched my car." She regretted that right to her toes, but it had been necessary. Still, she'd loved that car. "They'll find it soon if they haven't already. Just so you know."

"Thanks for telling me. I wouldn't have liked waiting while they sifted through the ashes looking for your bones."

"You'd have cared?"

"They're bones I once jumped. I'd have cared."

"Then prove it. Don't screw me on this," she said.

"You already said we couldn't do that again."

"You know what I mean. Sunny's a good person. And you gave in way too easily. Why?"

"Because Kiley loves her." Like that was proof of his loyalty. "You said Sunny hasn't accepted this yet. You think she's gonna try to come back? Resume her life here?"

"I think she might. If she does, she'll probably end up dead. But in case she doesn't, I don't to burn all her bridges. Not yet."

"The answer's obvious, you know. Somebody's gotta take out Brax Hayes. Or at least lock him up for good. He belongs behind bars more than anybody I ever met, in prison or out."

"You don't think I'd have done that by now if I could? The guy's Teflon. Stays squeaky clean. He's his father's heir apparent.

Daddy's lackeys think it's their job to protect him. They do all the golden boy's dirty work."

Jack said, "Well, he's here, himself, in Big Falls, so maybe he's decided to be more hands-on in this case."

"Yeah. With her, it's personal," Eve said.

"Why?"

Sunny opened the motel door and came back outside. "Eve?" she called, looking around.

Eve waved a hand, holding it higher than the open trunk. "I gotta go," she whispered. "Make sure Jason McIntyre knows she wasn't in the car."

"And how do you suggest I do that without inspiring him to beat me 'til I tell him how I know?"

"Use your imagination." She tapped off and dropped the phone into her pocket, closed the overnight bag, and then the trunk.

"Need any help?" Sunny asked.

"Nope, I was just sorting us out a night's worth. The less we bring in, the faster we can get out again. I put some of your stuff in my car, and some of mine in yours, just in case. Lucky for you, your big suitcase made it in here."

"How about my bathroom stuff?" she asked, hope and doubt etched equally on her face.

"Nope. But I always carry extra."

"You're like a Girl Scout, aren't you?"

"I'm like a girl Federal agent," Eve said. She closed the trunk and went into the room.

Jason didn't know what to do with himself. He'd been to Sunny's place, but there was no sign of Sunny, and a lot of her things were missing. Like she'd packed. Like she knew she was leaving him.

He and his brothers had checked all over town, asking everyone who knew her, but no one had a clue where she might've gone. It was like she'd vanished from the face of the earth.

She was in trouble. He knew it down deep in his bones. That trumped everything else. He could be mad at her for lying to him later. Demand an explanation for all of this later. But that took a back seat to her being okay. He had to help her. He had to make sure she was safe. It wasn't modern thinking, it wasn't thinking at all. His heart was calling the shots, not his head.

He'd finally convinced his brothers that he'd be okay if they returned to their lives and their wives. And since then he'd called Sunny's phone a hundred times. Nothing.

He clung to Jimmy's assurance that the police were looking for her and had more resources than he did. Jimmy said he should stick near home tonight, that Sunny would likely come back, because she'd left her car in his driveway. That made some kind of sense, but he wasn't gonna be able to comply.

His cell phone went off, which, at this time of night, meant something big. He glanced at it fast before answering, disappointed it wasn't Sunny calling. "Jimmy, you find her?"

"Jason...um. No. Not...look, there's no reason to think the worst, but–"

"I'm already thinking the worst so spit it out."

"Sorry. We found Eve's car out by the old Yancy Motor Lodge."

"Just the car? Anyone inside?"

"Well...we can't tell yet. The car...Jason, the car burned."

"Burned?" His heart almost beat through his chest. "What do you mean, burned, you mean...*burned*?" His heart jumped and started trying to pound its way out of his chest.

"We've got a team going over it. There's no point in you coming out here. I'll call you as soon as I know anything for sure."

"I'm coming out there." He disconnected, picked up his jacket and keys on the way out the door, jumped into his truck and drove through the darkest night he'd ever seen. His heart broke a little more with every mile. What if this was it? What if he'd lost Sunny forever?

He didn't *know* that, though. He didn't *know* Sunny was in the car when it burned. He didn't know anything, so he tried to hold it all in. And he did okay right up until he pulled over behind a half-dozen police and fire vehicles with strobing lights. He walked past them over cracked blacktop to the abandoned motel's parking lot. There were spotlights set up around it, aimed at a charred black frame that used to be a car. It felt like his heart fell straight to his feet, and his chest got all tight.

He ran closer, and when a cop he didn't know started up to him, Jimmy Corona said, "Hold off, hold off, that's Jason, that's my brother-in-law. He's okay." And the cop let him pass.

Jason stopped a couple of feet shy of the car. There was a woman closer, kneeling on the pavement in the spotlight's beam, dabbing ashes with Q-tips and gathering busted bits of taillight with tweezers. A man snapped photos from every angle.

Jason made himself look at the car, at the front seats, praying he wouldn't see two charred bodies there. But he didn't. There weren't even any seats left. Just ash and blackened springs. No seats, no dashboard, no steering wheel. Every bit of glass had shattered into fine shards and flown in a million directions. The back half of the car wasn't even car shaped. It was mostly missing.

"What happened?" he whispered.

"Looks like the gas tank exploded," the woman with the tweezers and bags said, without breaking her concentration.

Jimmy came to stand beside him. "There's no evidence anyone was in the car."

He looked his brother in law in the eyes. "Is there any evidence there wasn't?"

Jim's gaze shifted a little. "You've just gotta hang onto hope and give us some time."

He closed his eyes, turned away from the wreckage, and saw a car door lying all the way across the parking lot. Jimmy put a hand on his shoulder. "Let's go somewhere we can talk."

"I can't—"

"Just walk with me, Jay. We've learned a few things tonight."

That paused the horror clip of Sunny burning alive that was playing through Jason's mind. He walked away with Jimmy across the parking lot, away from everyone else, beyond reach of the lights.

"So, the guy who busted into your workshop is Landry Mason. He's got a record as long as my arm. Multiple assaults, conspiracy, weapons charges, harassment. He's a white supremacist known to run with a small, but violent hate group known as The Power."

"Hate group." Jason flashed on the swastika tattoo on Sunny's head.

"This group was unheard of until...you remember that car that drove into the protestors at Barrier Park, five, maybe six years ago?"

"Seven. I was still in Texas when that happened. That was them?" Jimmy nodded. "One of the protesters was killed, wasn't he?"

"Yeah, and another was paralyzed. A dozen more hurt in less permanent ways. The question I have is, what is a hate group doing in Big Falls?"

It was no coincidence, that was for sure. "Did you ask him that?"

"He's still unconscious. Lost a lot of blood. Could be brain damage."

Jason knew this was all tied to Sunny. The break-in, that

tattoo, Eve's sudden appearance and disappearance with Sunny in tow. It was all connected. He thought about telling Jimmy, then thought again. Maybe she wouldn't want him to know the thug had been calling her Mary. He needed to find out what it meant, first.

"What did a guy like that want with you?" Jimmy asked.

He shrugged, looked back at the car. "When will we know if she was—if they were in the car?"

"They'll rush the tests. This is no small deal. Eve DuVall was—"

"Is. Eve DuVall *is*."

"Is a federal agent. FBI."

Jason's brain went numb, he was that shocked. He couldn't even form words and wasn't sure what they would've been if he could.

Jimmy went on. "I thought Sunny was acting odd and I was suspicious Eve might be threatening her or something, so I looked into her."

"FBI," Jason said stupidly.

"Sunny never mentioned her old friend who worked for the FBI before?"

"Never. What's the FBI doing in Big Falls?"

"At first, I thought she was probably on vacation, visiting an old friend just like she says she is. FBI agents are people. They take vacations and visit old friends."

"But now?"

"Now, I think a guy like Landry Mason and an FBI Agent showing up here at the same time is damn unlikely to be coincidental."

"I gotta find Sunny."

"She probably got scared, with Landry lunging in there waving a gun around like that."

But Jason could tell that he thought there was more to it. He looked at the burnt car again, and then he thought about

Sunny's car, home in his driveway. Once Jimmy or the FBI figured out this all tied to her, they would probably impound it. He was surprised they hadn't already. He had to get to it first. Maybe some clue in the car would tell him where she might've gone. And why. And whether she'd been blown to bits on the way.

He gave one last look at the debris scattered all over the parking lot, wondering if Sunny was out there among it.

"Jason, there's nothing out there. We've been over it."

"I gotta go," Jason said. "I can't be here."

"I understand. I'll be in touch."

CHAPTER 11

*J*n the hours before sunrise, Jason was going through Sunny's car in the dark. With the door open, the interior lights stayed on, and his porch light helped a little. He was in the back seat where he'd found her cat carrier. Not surprising, since she'd been looking for Griselda until everything went crazy. But there was also a small suitcase. He unzipped it, pawed through the clothes inside, feeling guilty and doing it anyway. There was a plastic grocery bag stuffed in there, with all her personal stuff inside; makeup, hair products, soaps and creams and all that.

She'd planned to be away for more than one night, and she'd planned it *before* the maniac had attacked them. She hadn't run off due to trauma from witnessing him cleave a guy through the chest. She'd been planning to run off either way.

It was like the clouds parted in his brain. Suddenly the intensity of their lovemaking last night made sense. Goodbye-sex, that's what it was.

His heart sank. Could that mean she was planning to leave for good? She wouldn't, though. She *couldn't*. He moved to the front seat, and the first thing he saw was her purse on the floor, her cell phone in its front pocket in plain sight.

"No way, would she leave those. Not if she had a choice."

"Hey, there Jason. How are you, uh, holding up?"

Jack Kellogg was standing outside of Sunny's car looking at him, hands in his jeans pockets. Jason got out of the car, closed the door and looked at the guy. "Do you really care how I'm holding up, Jack?"

"You're family."

"I'm your son-in-law's brother."

"So, nephew-in-law, then? Something like that? I'm s'posed to care, right?"

"Yeah. You're s'posed to." He took a deep breath. "I've repeated the story until I'm hoarse, including to your daughter Kiley. Maybe you could get it from her and save me having to–"

"I'm not here for the story. I already know the story."

Jason swept the grief and the fog of twenty hours without sleep from his mind. Jack was standing there in his driveway at four in the morning. "You seem to know a little more about all this than you ought to. You were contradicting me last night when I said I thought the attack was random, and that Sunny wasn't in danger."

"That's 'cause it *wasn't* random, and she *is* in danger. But she wasn't in the car. That's what I came to tell you."

"What car?"

"Eve's car. What's left of it."

Jason let that digest for a second, then he took a step closer. "What do you know about this?"

Jack held up both hands. "The only thing I know is that Eve and Sunny were *not* in the car when it burned. They're safe. Or they were two hours ago."

Jason grabbed the front of his shirt. "*How* do you know?"

"Eve called and told me so."

"Why the hell would she tell you anything?"

Jack looked down, looked up again. "Let go of my shirt."

Jason was out of line and he knew it. He let go. He was not a violent man, until lately. He tried to calm down and reminded himself that Jack was Kiley's father, little Diana's grandpa. He slowed and deepened his breaths of the cool, dry air and listened to the cicadas chirping out in the scrub lot behind his place.

Jack smoothed his shirt, gave it a tug, took a step back. "Eve and I are old friends. She said Sunny wouldn't want you to worry when they found the car, and asked me to help out."

"You wanna help out, you can tell all this to the police. Along with who the hell burned the car, and why, and where Eve and Sunny are, and why some white nationalist moron would want to shoot her." He pulled out his phone to call Jimmy back.

"Yeah," Jack said. "A, I can't do any of that because I don't know shit and B—"

"They can track the phone she called from."

"And B," Jack continued. "It was a burner phone. She tossed it as soon as we hung up. However, I do have a suggestion."

"Jack, I swear to God, if you don't tell me everything you know—"

"I could, and that would take time, and when I finished, you'd decide to go after them. I figure it's more efficient if we skip the me-telling-you part, and go straight to the us-going-after-them part."

He rolled his eyes and started to turn away, but Jack grabbed his arm. When he turned, the older man looked him right in the eyes. His were pale blue, and crystal clear, and they appeared sincere. "One thing I know for sure is that they're in trouble, Jason. So how about you quit wasting time and go throw a few things in a bag so we can try to catch up to 'em?"

"How do we know where to look for them?"

"I know *exactly* where to look for them," he said. "Eve is good, but I'm better."

"Why?" Jason said. "Why do you want to help me?"

"I don't. I want to help Eve. And I figure if I help Sunny out, maybe I make something up to Kiley." He looked a little embarrassed, but covered it fast.

That, that expression just then, was genuine. That was how Jason read it, anyway. Maybe he was just desperate, but he chose to believe Jack. "I'll get my stuff. Wait here. I won't be five minutes."

"Your hospitality is overwhelming."

"Don't touch anything," Jason said, and then he went inside.

He did just what Jack said, throwing some essentials and a change of clothes into a bag. While he was doing it, he flipped through his wallet, found the card Angie had given him, and tapped the number into his phone. It only rang once.

"Everett Investigations, this is Riley. How can I help you?"

"This is Jason McIntyre," he said. "I'm—"

"Jason. Angie said you might be calling. She told me everything she knows, which isn't much. Need me to start looking for Sunny?"

"I need you to start looking *into* Sunny."

"Holy... All right. Okay. First, you need to tell me everything you know," she said. "Even the stuff you didn't tell the cops. My sister and Kiley are sure you're keeping things back."

"They're wrong."

"I work for *you*. None of it will go any further."

"Not even to your sister-in-law?"

"I'm a professional."

He made a snap decision to trust her—to an extent. "I only have a few minutes. I'll have to talk fast. The guy who came in here wasn't after me, he was after Sunny, only he called her Mary."

"Mary?"

"His name is Landry Mason and he's with a white nationalist group called The Power."

"Got it. I'll run a background check on him. What else?"

"A woman named Eve DuVall showed up in town out of nowhere the day all this started, claiming to be Sunny's old friend. Turns out she's FBI."

"FBI?"

"And right after the attack, she and Eve took off. She left her car. Her purse. She left her freaking phone, Riley."

"Okay. Okay."

He took a calming breath, tried to get a grip on himself. His heart was racing again. "Jack Kellogg knows something about this. Says Eve called to tell him they weren't in her burned-out car, which was just found—"

"I know about the car."

"He wants to come with me to look for them. Says he's knows where they're heading."

"So just to be clear, this is Kendra and Kiley's father Jack Kellogg?"

"The same. You've met him?"

"Never had the pleasure. Know *of* him, though."

"Through your work?" Had Jack been keeping his nose clean?

"I keep my finger on the pulse of Big Falls."

"Our little town hasn't let go of you yet, has she, Riley?" It wasn't really a question.

"I don't think she ever will. Did Jack say *how* he knows where they're going?"

"Not yet. He's being cagey. Makes me nervous."

"You're smart to be nervous. From what I hear, that guy put the artist in con-artist. Keeping him close is probably the best way to keep an eye on him, though. Just be careful, and stay in touch."

"I will. Gotta go." He pocketed the phone, grabbed his bag and headed outside. "We'll take my truck," he said, opening the driver's door. "Hop in and tell me which way."

"Southwest," Jack said. He climbed into the passenger seat. "Eve has a little place in New Mexico that nobody knows about."

"Then how do you know about it?"

He smiled, dimples forming, blue eyes sparkling, but he didn't answer.

~

Sunny rolled over in the strange bed, absently stroking Griz with her toes. The cat was stretched out and snoring softly. Who ever heard of a cat who snored? At least she was sleeping. Sunny was wide awake with no sign of sleep in sight. It was six a.m. They'd got to bed by three, but she hadn't closed her eyes once.

The motel's address was printed on the complimentary notepad beside the telephone. They were only a couple of hours from Big Falls, even though they'd driven all day. Eve had been taking them in circles, looping back and forth, heading in different directions, all just to confuse anyone who might be following them. So, they hadn't gone far. They were cutting across a corner of Texas, heading toward New Mexico.

Everything in her was screaming that this was wrong. Big Falls was her home. It couldn't be right for her to run away.

She looked around the room as if for an answer. Eve lay curled on her side in the other bed, sound asleep as far as Sunny could tell. Sure, *she* could sleep. It wasn't *her* life being turned upside down.

Creeping quietly out of bed in borrowed pajamas—white cotton with pale blue piping—she didn't even wake Griz. And she was careful not to wake Eve, either.

She tiptoed to the dresser to slip the room key into the PJ top's pocket, answering the age-old question, why put pockets in pajamas, then moved silently to the door. Normally, on nights when she couldn't sleep or any time she was stressed out, she baked. She'd baked her way through her hate-filled childhood. She'd baked madly during her awakening at college. She'd baked her way through love and loss, through betraying her own father, and through running for her life from his wrath.

She twisted the door in slow motion, watching Eve the whole time, then ducked through the smallest opening possible and closed the door as slowly as she'd opened it. Then she walked out across the parking lot.

Baking was comfort to her. It was control. It was creating something wonderful from parts that weren't much on their own. Who would eat a spoonful of flour? But when you added sparkling sugar and rich, real butter and a couple of eggs, you had the beginnings of anything. Anything at all, depending on proportions and what else you put in. Cookies and cakes and tarts and tortes and breads and muffins and....

She couldn't bake tonight. There were no parts she could put together. Her life was out of her control. Braxton was the one mixing ingredients in her life now. Hatred. Violence. Vengeance. He was poisoning the batter.

She'd never wanted to taste those flavors again. But instead of escaping them, she'd brought them straight to Big Falls, the closest thing to paradise this side of heaven. She'd brought them straight to Jason, the finest man she'd ever known.

She'd put him in danger. And there wasn't a thing that would stop her from warning him now. Eve said she'd taken care of that, but Sunny had to be certain. She couldn't bear the thought of him in her brother's sites. Nor could she let him believe for a second that she'd burned to death in Eve's car.

She walked across the parking lot to the motel's office. Its light was on, an orange neon VA ANN Y sign. Both Cs were blown out and the V was flickering. It buzzed intermittently. The air felt good. Cool, with a hint of moisture. Winter in the southwest wasn't cold. It just a break from the heat.

She went through the door into the motel office and a bell jangled. No one was behind the chest-high desk. It was wood, painted white, with a terra-cotta tiled surface. There were cacti shaped wall hangings and a parade of chili peppers danced across the top the clay-red walls.

A sign said, OFFICE CLOSED—RING BELL FOR SERVICE.

The space in front of the counter was jam-packed with things for the convenience of the guests. A coffee maker stood on a table beside a bag of ground roast, powdered creamer, all manner of sweeteners in colorful packets. There was a toaster oven and a case full of cellophane-wrapped baked goods. She shuddered.

There was a rack of roadmaps and flyers right beside a cordless landline phone with a "Guest use only" sign underneath it. She'd planned to ask to use a phone, even though she knew Eve wouldn't like it.

Sure, caller ID would identify where she was. But they would only be here for another hour or two. They'd move on again as soon as Eve got up.

She picked up the phone and dialed the number she knew by heart. Jason's number. She imagined he'd be sleeping. It was almost 6 a.m., but still dark outside. February days were still short.

She expected a sexy, sleepy "hello?" after several rings.

Instead he picked up in half a ring and barked his greeting, startling the her.

"It's me," she said, bringing the phone back to her ear.

"Sunny! Jeeze, Sunny, are you okay? Where are you?"

"Jason, you're not safe. That guy you killed wasn't alone. He's part of a group—"

"I know."

"You have to be careful."

"Where are you?"

"I can't...I want to, but I can't tell you. You'll come after me, and it's not safe. I'll be okay. Eve will make sure I'm okay. And maybe...when this is over, somehow I can–"

"Hello there, baby sister."

Brax's voice came from behind her, and she could've sworn an icy frost spread up her spine.

"Sunny?" Jason was alarmed. "Who is that? Sunny! Dammit, answer me."

Brax walked up behind her, reached around and took the phone from her ear. She only saw his hand. He had sausage fingers, pudgy palms. He depressed the cutoff, and dropped the phone on the floor.

"Turn around," he said. And she did, because there was no reason not to. She was just as dead either way. Maybe it would be harder for him to pull the trigger if he was looking her in the eye.

He looked the same, only older, a little fatter. He had a round face, big round eyes, like little boy eyes, set just a tad too close together. Light blue. Blond lashes. Dirty blond hair that seemed almost brown the way he wore it, hedgehog style, with gel.

"Long time, no see."

There was beer on his breath. But when had there ever not been? He had his hunting knife in his hand. She'd recognize its wooden handle and a fat silver blade forever. She saw it in her nightmares.

CHAPTER 12

"Sunny?" Jason said into the phone. "Sunny, what's going on, who is that? Sunny!" The call ended. "Dammit!"

"What'd she say, what's going on?"

"She's in trouble." Jason passed his cell phone to Jack. "Caller ID said Courtside Motor Lodge. Google the address."

Jason pushed the truck up to 85.

Jack had said that Eve would head southwest, so they'd been driving southwest for two hours now. He'd refused to say how he knew, or thought he knew, or why he thought they had any chance of catching up when the girls had such a big head start.

"We won't be any help if you roll this thing, Jason."

"I'm not gonna roll this thing." He let up just a little, though. Because yes, he was.

"There are six Courtside Motor Lodges within a hundred miles," Jack said.

"Check the phone number. Area code and exchange."

Jack tapped the phone. "Got it. Ten twenty-nine Eckhart Road, el Fuego, New Mexico. I told you so." Jack flashed his dimples and gave a nod.

"How far?"

"Hang on, hang on." He tapped his phone again. "Seven point two miles."

Jason looked at him slowly. "You're kidding me."

"What can I say? When I'm good, I'm good."

"I guess maybe you are. Let's get there."

He pushed the pedal harder. "It sounded like someone came in. There was a man's voice. I didn't hear any sign of Eve. She's supposed to be protecting her. Where the hell is she?"

"Good question."

"Who's after Sunny, Jack?"

Jack looked up from his phone. "Her brother."

Sunny couldn't believe she was standing there, staring into her brother's eyes. And for a moment, she flashed back to the last time she'd seen him.

Their father's trial was over. Braxton would be tried separately, as an accomplice, but it didn't matter. Her testimony was already on record. The evidence already in the DA's hands. She'd told them where to find her father's laptop, the one he kept hidden. The one he used to run his group, and to record all his conversations, in case he needed something to hold over someone's head. Blackmail material. The idiot never considered he was also recording evidence against himself.

She remembered the soundbite they'd played in court, the one where her father had ordered his boys to find Dave Barron in that crowd of protestors, and mow him down.

You don't leave until he's dead, and you make sure Mary sees it happen. I don't want her to forget. Not ever.

That had convicted him. There was no question in the juror's minds once they heard him give the order. Even though the investigators had never found out who was driving the car, they knew who'd given the order and why. It was a hate crime. Dave had been targeted for dating a white girl. By her father.

She had been in the courtroom to hear the guilty verdict, and to see her father taken away in shackles. And she hadn't felt an ounce of regret. She'd done the right thing. She'd done the right thing for Dave.

She left the courthouse to walk to a local restaurant, and her cell phone rang. It was Eve. "Congratulations! But we're not done yet. We need to get you out of town. Your brother—"

"I can handle my brother. I told you, I don't want to go into witness protection."

"Braxton is a dangerous man," Eve said. "Far more dangerous than your father. He's smarter. And he's not behind bars yet."

Unlike her father, her brother had been released on bond until his trial.

"I'm smarter than either of them," she told Eve. "I'm fine. I promise."

"We still on for dinner?"

"I'm on my way now. Patrick's on Eaton, right? I'm a block away."

"Good. See you soon."

Mary put the phone in her pocket, and then a gloved hand came over her face, a car skidded to a stop at her side, its back door popped open, and she was shoved in, all in the space of a heartbeat. She landed face down on the seat, and the guy got in behind her and barked "Drive!" while crushing her face to the upholstery, hand on the back of her neck.

"No point fighting, Sis. I win. I always win." Her brother. Braxton.

She stopped fighting him, focused on inching the phone out of her pocket underneath her body, pressing her thumbprint to the button. She couldn't see the screen, couldn't lift her head. They hit a bump, and she pretended it rocked her right off the seat, onto the floor, getting the glimpse she needed to tap the phone icon, and then her most recent call. She shoved the phone under the seat while Brax yanked her onto the seat by her hair, then started pawing her coat pockets, ripping the fabric.

She twisted against his groping paws. "God, get off me, what do you want?"

Satisfied her pockets were empty, he reached down to the floor, and she almost panicked, until he came up with her purse, turned it upside down and shook its contents all over the seat between them. At least he had to slide over to do it. He took her wallet, emptied it of cash, stuffed it into his denim jacket's pocket. "Not gonna need that where you're going." Then he pulled out his fat hunting knife. He'd burned his initials into its handle. He grabbed a fistful of her hair, and she gasped and fought, but he just wrapped it around his fist and pulled, and then he brought the knife to it and started sawing.

She kicked and twisted, but he just yanked harder. "I can pull it out or hack it off. Your call."

"You're sick, Braxton!"

"I'm sick? You're the one who turned on your own blood, Mary." And he kept on sawing with that thick knife. Cutting and pulling, and smiling the whole time. His eyes were alive, sparkling. He loved what he was doing. He cut it all the way through, and then he took her hair, all wrapped around his fist, and he threw it out the window, wiggling his fingers to let the wind take every strand.

She reached up to touch her head, but he grabbed her wrist before she could. The car had slowed. It pulled through an open overhead garage door into a small building, and stopped. The place looked abandoned. An old tool bench along one wall, a rusting iron vise still attached, a couple of tires in the corner. A tool cart lay on its side on the cracked concrete floor.

The two guys in the front seat, Landry Mason and the one she knew only as Major, got out. Landry closed the overhead door, and it was pitch dark. She smelled old motor oil and was more afraid than she'd ever been in her life. Brax opened the car door and hauled her out, holding her wrist. She tried to get her legs under her, but he moved too fast so she stumbled and he dragged her.

A light came on so suddenly she had to close her eyes.

Someone stood the cart up, and Braxton picked her up and slammed her onto it. The raised metal lip around its edge bit into her back. Then Brax took her chin in his hand, twisting her head to one side. "You'll wanna be real still for this," he said, and he took that damned knife and scraped it over the already tender spot where he'd hacked off her hair.

"Ow! Dammit, Brax, you're cutting me."

"Not yet, I'm not." He scraped some more, then said, "Gimme the gun."

Her blood went cold. "You had to shave me to shoot me? What the hell, Braxton?"

"Not that kind of gun, Sis." He lifted his hand, and the tool he held buzzed. Tattoo gun, she realized, as he started drilling ink into her scalp.

The nightmarish memory played out all at once, a flash, a download. And she was in the present again, there with her brother, looking at him for the first time in six years. His face was that kind of puffy that only came from hard drinking. His cheeks and nose looked like he stood outside in a blizzard every day. But he'd never seen snow, as far as she knew. He was thirty-two. He looked fifty.

"You didn't think you could just run away from who you are, did you? From your family? From your past?"

"Hoped," she said. "Only hoped."

"You killed our father."

"He died in prison."

"You put him there!"

She nodded, her eyes on him, on the knife she knew too well. Her scalp flinched in remembered pain. And then she saw Eve through the glass door behind her brother. Eve put a finger to her lips.

Then she kicked the door open. It hit Braxton in the back, which had not been her intention. It sent him lurching forward, blade first. Sunny spun to one side, and threw herself past him, crashing into Eve's legs and taking her out. Eve landed hard as headlights bounded into the parking lot. Her gun skittered across the pavement. She rolled and scrambled after it. Brax lurched to his feet and out the door. He got to the gun first, grabbed it up, then shielded his eyes because of the truck's headlights blazing into them.

From those lights, a shout. "Get away from them!"

"Jason." She hadn't meant to blurt his name on a breath of panic. He couldn't be here. But he was out of the truck, facing down her brother. "Jason, don't! He has a gun."

Jason stepped out of the glare, put one hand on the side of his truck, and sprang up over the side into the back, where he ducked low. She thought her heart stopped when he did that. God, Brax could've shot him.

"I'm not gonna let you kill him, Brax. You'll have to kill me first."

"That's kind of the plan." He aimed the gun at her.

She could feel it on her. Her flesh tightened where the barrel aimed. She was shaking.

"Come on out of that truck, cowboy." Braxton grabbed for her, but she dodged, so he pointed his gun at her instead. "Come on out or I just shoot her now."

"Don't!" she shouted. "He'll shoot me either way! It's what he came for."

Her brother smiled, cocked his head to one side. "She's got a point." And then he looked at her and tilted his head until he could look right down the barrel. And she could look up the barrel, right into his baby blue eye.

"Bye, Sis."

Something flew into him. No, someone. Jason! He came leaping out of nowhere hitting Braxton like a missile. They landed on the pavement together and the gun went flying.

Lights were popping on in motel room windows.

They rolled apart and sprang to their feet. Jason had a freaking sword in his hand, and her brother had picked up something like a tire iron. He swung it like a cave man swinging a club. Jason moved like water, though, reshaping himself to avoid every blow. He wasn't trying too hard to inflict harm. Going through the motions, keeping Brax off balance and jumping backward again and again.

She picked up the gun and aimed it. "Stop!" The volume and depth of her voice reverberated and brought the men to a standstill. Eve, too, who'd been creeping up on her from the left.

Sunny put the site on her brother's chest, and her finger touched the safety. Already off. Brax froze, and she looked right into his eyes for a second. He knew she could do it. And *she* knew she could do it. She lowered her cheek to her shoulder and looked down the site at his widest point, right between the shoulders.

"Sunny, let me take that gun from you, now." Eve sidled up to her.

"I've gotta do it, Eve," she whispered. "He's never gonna stop. He was driving that car, I know he was. He killed Dave. He'll kill Jason. He'll kill me."

"You don't want to spend the rest of your life in prison. You know you don't want that. He's not worth that."

"Jason's worth that." She straightened her arms, re-focused her aim, called out, "Step away from him, Jason."

"Sunny, what are you doing?" Jason asked. "Eve, arrest him or something, huh? He tried to kill her."

A new blaze of headlights blinded her as three more jacked-up vehicles roared up on them. One stopping right in between Sunny and her brother and Jason. Its door opened and closed. Eve swept the gun from her hand as the truck sped away again. Sunny blinked in the dark. Her brother was gone and Jason was on the ground, facedown.

"No." She ran to him as the other pickups fishtailed into the road and sped away, falling to her knees, sobbing and holding him, overcome with panic. "Jason, no. No, no, no, no!"

He pushed himself up, twisting around and grabbing her shoulders. "Hey, look at me. I'm okay. I'm okay."

She pressed her palms to his face and looked at him. "You're not dead."

"No, I'm not dead. Got dragged a few feet is all. Sunny are *you* okay?"

She blinked, nodded. He got up on his feet, and, taking her hands, helped her up onto hers.

She didn't feel like her knees were going to hold her. Everything solid in her had dissolved when she'd seen him on the ground. The past had come rushing back to engulf her, like living that horror all over again.

Then Jason just wrapped her in his arms. "Damn, I'm glad to see you in one piece."

"How did you... What are you doing here?"

"Where did you think I'd be? Sunny, whatever else, you're in trouble. Clearly." He released her and looked past her, into the motel office. It wasn't wrecked, but there were a hellish number of flyers scattered. "I came to help."

"You can't help," she told him. Then turned to Eve. Jack Kellogg was standing there talking to her. "We have to go."

"I know you were faking amnesia," Jason said. "I know you're hiding from your past, and hiding your history from me and everyone else in Big Falls."

"Did Jack come with you?"

"Yeah."

"What are you doing with him?" She dropped her voice to a whisper. "You know he can't be trusted."

"He knew where you and Eve were going."

"That's *not* good news."

"I wouldn't have got here in time if not for him."

"You could've been killed."

"So could you. So could she."

"It's her job. And my problem. I'm not gonna let you make it yours, Jason." She walked up to Eve, and the two of them started toward the room. Its door was closed, but several others were open, with people looking out.

"It's all good," Jack said to the curious motel guests, flashing his smile. "Bunch of drunken rednecks looking for trouble. They're gone now."

The doors closed one by one.

Eve shot her a look as they walked. "What the hell were you doing out here alone?"

"Whatever I want, Eve. You don't control me."

"I'm not trying to control you, I'm trying to keep you alive."

"It's my life. Maybe I should get to decide how best to preserve it."

Eve's face changed. It went sort of lax, and her eyes rounded, losing the angry squint. "He knows where we are. He found us, Sunny. And I don't know how. There's no way he followed, but if he did it once, he'll do it again."

"Maybe not," Jack said.

They stopped walking and turned. Jason and Jack were right behind them. Jack shrugged and said, "If we get out of here before they get a chance to regroup, we have a jump start. Did you cut him, do you think?" he asked Jason.

Jason shuddered. "I'm not real fond of using my swords to kill people. But yeah. He'll need a few stitches."

"Good, that'll take time," Jack said. "So, if we leave now–"

Eve said, "What is all this 'we' stuff, Jack?" She couldn't seem to hold his steady gaze, so she paced to the road instead. "They headed north."

"But they'll turn around. They already know we're heading southwest," Sunny said. "Probably the same way Jack did."

Jack sent Eve a half-smile, like an inside joke.

"Definitely not the same way Jack did," Eve said without inflection. "We'll head east."

"I think we should head home." Jason walked up to Sunny and put a hand on her shoulder. "Look, you've lied to me the whole time we've been together, Sunny, and I'm not over that. I don't know if I can *get* over that." He shook his head. "But even so, I know you. I *know you*, Sunny. And I know you belong in Big Falls. Running away isn't the answer."

"Sometimes it's the only answer," she said. "It was an answer for me once, and it lasted for six years. I had a great life as Sunny Cantrell. But it's over now."

"Just like that? Isn't your life in Big Falls worth fighting for?"

"Yeah, if it was a fight I could win. But it's not, and other people will get dragged into it. They'll get hurt. They'll die. You'll die, Jason."

"Come on, nobody's gonna die."

"People already have."

They stared at each other for a long moment. She didn't know what was in his eyes, all she could see in them was searching. He wanted her secrets. His eyes were mining for them, and she had to look away.

Eve finally broke the tension. "We can't just sit here and wait for Brax and his boys to regroup. Let's get the cat and our crap out of the room and get moving. Any direction is better than no direction."

"East," Sunny said. "Back into Texas." And a little bit closer to Big Falls, just to see if it might ease this stretched rubber band feeling she'd had since they'd left her dusty roads behind. It was homesickness, that was all. It would pass. She wasn't going back. She wasn't going to pollute the place with her family's toxic cloud.

～

Jason waited with Jack until the women came out of their motel room. Eve had a bag slung over her shoulder. Sunny's hair was combed, all over to one side to cover the bandaged spot and evil tattoo. She wore jeans, a T-shirt that clung to her curves, and a denim jacket, and small round sunglasses. Sunny Cantrell didn't dress like that, unless she was maybe planning to do some free-hand plumbing. Like that time last summer with the leaky pipe. He'd found her in the basement in overalls, a Rosie the Riveter band around her hair. He remembered the smudge on her cheek and the frustration in her eyes.

This was a different Sunny.

He'd thought for a minute back there that she might shoot the guy. Her brother. Imagine that. Imagine there being so much anguish in a family that a man could try to kill his own sister. Or that a woman could shoot her own brother.

It really had looked possible for a few seconds. Her eyes had been cold, and her finger, softly wrapped around the trigger. She'd closed one eye and for just an instant he knew it was about to happen. She was going to do it.

Then those boys in the pickups had shown up.

This was a hidden part she'd never shown him, a shadow side that was maybe eclipsing her light right now. There was no bounce in this Sunny's step. No light in her eyes. Something cold had quenched the flame. She seemed hard, this Sunny. Her joy was gone.

"Jack knows a place we can hole up," he said, when she caught him staring.

"A hunting cabin," Jack put in. "No one around for miles. Great cell reception, due to the elevation. We can hole up there, get some rest and figure out a plan."

"We already have a plan," Eve said.

Sunny looked at her, held her eyes and said, "No we don't."

"Sunny, listen–"

"I know, Eve. I know the deal. New name, new life…but that means killing the old one." Sunny reached back into the room for the cat carrier. Griz lay inside, growling. "Either your way or Braxton's way, Sunny's just as dead." She shifted her eyes and they locked with Jason's. "There's got to be another option. I just…I need time to figure out what it is."

Jason nodded with his eyes. "Good for you, Sunny." Then he glanced at Jack. "What if we split up, take different routes, and meet at the cabin? We'll have time to regroup and come up with a better plan there."

Sunny hefted the cat carrier into the back seat of Eve's car, then closed the door. She had a small backpack over her shoulder as she rejoined the group.

"I'll ride with Eve," Jack said. "Your maniac brother is more likely to follow her car, since that's what he's been doing."

"We weren't followed," Eve said. "Not by line of sight anyway. I'm too good to be followed." She looked at Sunny and said, "But he's right. That'll get you out of his crosshairs for a little while."

"I won't let you be my decoy, Eve–"

"It's my job, Sunny. I get paid for this, and I'm damn good at it."

"She's the best," Jack added, getting into Eve's car, passenger side.

"And I've got back-up a phone call away," Eve added, and she got behind the wheel, started it up and drove away.

Sunny still hadn't moved.

"Come on." Jason held out a hand.

She stared at it. "It's not the same, Jason. *I'm* not the same."

"I am very clear on that."

Her eyes shifted up to meet his. The woman looking back at him was a Sunny he'd never met before. He'd never thought she was anything more than sweetness and light. But there was much more to her than that.

And then she said, "They've got my cat!"

"Don't you trust Eve to take care of her?"

CHAPTER 13

*J*ason watched Sunny get into the passenger side of his truck, slipping off her backpack on the way. She'd ridden in that seat beside him a thousand times. And yet this time felt entirely different.

She pulled her seatbelt on.

"When we first met, you never buckled up," he said.

"You were always nagging me about it."

"It worked." He nodded at her seatbelt.

"Nice normal people use their seatbelts," she said softly. "And that's who I was trying to be. Nice. Normal."

He was reforming his picture of who Sunny was, expanding the image to fit in every new piece she revealed. He thought he knew her, knew who she *really* was. Down deep. There might be stark differences between who she'd been before Big Falls and who'd she'd been *in* Big Falls, and who she was now.

But he thought he knew her heart. He knew her soul. The rest was just... depth perception.

"So how far is this cabin of Jack's?" she asked.

"Two hundred and thirty miles."

"That's a *drive*."

"It's a drive and a half, with the route we're taking."

"That's a lot of car time."

"Truck time," he corrected, tuning the dial to a mellow country station, and adjusting the volume low. He tried to gauge her mood by her face.

"You and your truck." The old Sunny beamed out for just a second when she smiled. And then she stopped herself.

But he'd seen it. He'd seen the old Sunny, his Sunny. She wasn't gone. She hadn't been an act or a game. She'd been real. She still was.

"We could talk," he said. "You could tell me about your past. Before Big Falls."

She took a deep nasal breath and nodded. "I'm working up to it. For now, suffice it to say I was a horrible person, born into a horrible family. And then one day I wasn't." She cranked up the radio.

He drove the first three hours, then had to stop for gas. "I have a limited amount of cash, but we can get a sandwich or something," he said.

"I have an unlimited amount of cash," Sunny said. "Well, my entire savings. I cashed everything out. I know how all this works."

"You've done it before. You did it when you came to Big Falls."

She nodded and got out. "Pump gas. I'll get food. I need the restroom anyway. Then I'll drive for a while." She walked away.

"Is your real name Mary Hayes?"

She stopped walking, but didn't turn around. "It was once." And then she continued into the convenience store.

He pulled out his phone, kind of reluctantly looking at the screen. There were fifty-two texts from the family loop. Jimmy's messages came from both his chief of police and step-brother-in-law capacities.

He skimmed past them all, stopping when he came to one from Riley Everett and tapping it.

It was long.

"Mary Sunlight Hayes, that's her real name. Three arrests, no convictions. Charges were unlawful assembly, resisting arrest, destruction of public property. All happened at white nationalist rallies. She was on the wrong side of those, I hate to tell you."

There was a photo next. A young girl, maybe sixteen, head shaved on one side and died black on the other. She wore black eyeliner and a "white pride" T shirt and stood near the front of a crowd of ignorant buffoons waving torches and racist signs. Idiots.

She was Sunny, that girl. And yet she wasn't. Her eyes were angry, but behind the anger, hollow, almost soulless.

A chill went through him. He shivered, it was so real. This was not the woman he knew. God, this was surreal, he felt like he'd fallen into some alternate reality where the most wholesome person in all of Big Falls was...was this. This angry teenage hate-monger.

He had to scroll past the photo just to stop looking at it. Riley had written more. "Her father was the head of a hate group called The Power. He was convicted for ordering his followers to drive a car into a group of protestors, killing a young man who had been targeted, specifically. Her brother, Braxton, was convicted of a lesser charge in connection with the same crime. He was the top suspect for driving the car, but there wasn't enough evidence to prove it. He did his time for harassment, assault, etc. Then he took over as leader of his father's group. Mary falls off the map after her father's murder conviction, before her brother's trial. I'm digging into that. More soon."

He texted back "Thanks" and then deleted the conversation, photo and all. He never wanted to see that thing again.

He pumped diesel into his truck, and watched through the store's wide front windows, catching glimpses of Sunny every now and then.

Eventually she came out, loaded down with two plastic shopping bags, a large fast food bag, and two gigantic cups of coffee.

He replaced the pump handle, then the gas cap, and then he wiped his hands on the provided paper towels before relieving her of some of her load, and opening the door for her.

She set her bounty on the seat between them and he drove the truck to the parking lot behind the building, out of sight from the highway. Sunny started unpacking his favorite McDonald's combo, like they used to do every now and then while running errands together in Tucker Lake.

She'd got her usual, too.

He put their coffee cups into the cup holders. "I really need you to tell me."

She closed her eyes, lowered her head. She nodded at the food. "I know I do. Eat your sandwich. We've gotta go."

"Yeah. We do." He ate his sandwich.

She ate hers, too, then they hit the highway while the fries were still warm.

She looked at him. He kept steeling sideways glances, to find her eyes on his face. Still working up to it, he thought.

Then she said, "My mother used to hold me and dance me around the room singing Little Mary Sunlight. That was my name. Mary Sunlight Hayes. I had a baby brother, Braxton. But my mother died before he learned to walk. I was never told how. She got sick and she died. End of story. My father had this group of friends who got together all the time and drank beer and complained about the state of the world. It evolved into a white nationalist group. My father was its leader."

"Did you believe in it?"

"I believed what my father told me. I went to the rallies. I did everything I could to win his approval. But the whole time, I had another life, a secret life of my own. I had my softball for part of the year. And the rest of the time, I baked. Inside my head, I pretended to be my mother, a nice, normal person. The kind who baked cookies and pies."

"The kind who wears pastel skirts and little sweaters with pearl buttons," he said.

"You notice everything, don't you?"

"No. No, I never noticed how much of you I wasn't seeing."

She sighed, was quiet for a moment. Then she said, "When I went to college, the blinders came off."

"I bet that was a shocker."

"Oh my God, yes. So many people. All different kinds, but not really. The big reveal was that they were all the same. Kids away from their families for the first time, going through the same slow awakening I was. All of us, really, realizing there are other ways to see the world besides the way our parents had. I think maybe that's the biggest thing you learn at college. How to think for yourself. So I did, and I woke up. I woke up hard."

He was watching her, watching the memories play across her face. "I'm surprised your father even let you go."

"I got a scholarship. He forbade me, but I got away from him long enough to register, and before classes began, I'd turned eighteen. There was nothing he could do after that."

"That was brave. What kind of scholarship?"

"Softball."

"I'd have bet it was academic."

"I was a pitcher. I was good."

"I don't doubt it." He smiled at her, and she smiled back, but then bit her lip.

"I fell for the pitcher on the baseball team. His name was Dave Barron."

139

"Why is that name familiar?" Then he remembered. "Wasn't that the name of the protestor who was killed in Barrier Park?"

She was nodding, but her eyes were far away. "My father ordered it. I was there with him, a big protest march against inequality. He was standing right beside me, and then the car just plowed him into a tree. He was just rocketed away on the nose of a car, until the tree stopped it. I looked at him, and he looked back and then his eyes just blinked out. And he was gone. The car backed up fast and he fell. People were screaming and running. The car pulled a donut and sped away."

"My God."

She snapped out of the past, locked her eyes onto his. "When I saw you on the ground back there it was like living through my worst nightmare all over again. Only this time it wasn't Dave. It was you. Dead because of me."

He pulled the truck over, turned toward her. "Not because of you," he said. "None of this is because of you."

"I helped the FBI get my dad," she said. "I told him where he kept the secret laptop, the one nobody was allowed to touch, in the wall behind his headboard. And they found it."

"You must've been scared to death."

"That's the thing, I wasn't. I told Eve I didn't need relocation, a new identity. I thought I'd be okay. But they didn't get enough evidence to prove it was Braxton driving that car. He and Landry wore ski masks and latex gloves. They ditched the car, didn't leave a hair or a fingerprint. But I knew it was him. I looked up from Dave's broken body. I looked right into his eyes, and he looked into mine from that ski mask just before he took off, spitting clumps of sod and grass and soil all over me. All over Dave."

"Sunny—"

"You should've let me shoot him, Jason."

"You weren't gonna shoot him."

"Yes, I was. That's the thing, you don't know me. Not really. I

140

was going to kill him because it's him or me. And maybe it's him or you, now that you killed his best friend.

"Landry's not dead. Not yet, and not far from it, but not dead. And I'm glad, because I don't want to carry someone's life on my conscience. Not even someone as bad as Mason Landry or your brother."

"Why not? What if killing him could save a dozen lives? Or a hundred?"

"It's not my call, that's why not. When it's his time to go, he'll go. It's not up to me."

She lowered her head. "You're the one who said I should fight for my life in Big Falls."

"And now I'm saying there's a way to fight for your life without taking his. And we'll find it, if you'll just let me help you." He cupped her face in his hands, cradling her chin, and then in spite of himself, he leaned down to kiss her.

She kissed him back, clasped his head, and kissed him silly. Then she jerked away, and slammed herself back into her seat. "Just drive."

"I'm driving."

"Don't do that again, Jason."

"Um, me? I came in for a comforting peck, and you tried to swallow my tongue, so..."

She lowered her head, her cheeks going red just like he'd known they would. "Don't know you," he muttered. "Shoot, I know you better than you do."

Eve glanced sideways at the most detestable man on the planet. And one of the most attractive. His lies flowed smoother than twenty-year-old whiskey and his eyes would sparkle the whole time. Those baby blues testified to the purity of his soul. There was sincerity in the depths of his dimples. It all came off as real.

And none of it was.

He was a snake charmer. And she was a cobra who'd landed herself right in his basket.

"How did you do it?" she asked.

"How did I do what?" He looked up from the roadmap, which he'd managed to open fully and refold to a manageable size showing just the section he wanted.

"Who the hell uses roadmaps anymore? There's a GPS in the dash."

"There's one in my phone, too," he said. "And in yours. And in your watch. And probably in your ass, given who you work for."

"Watch your mouth. How did you find us?"

"I like to see the big picture. The dashboard thingie only shows your current location and immediate surroundings. I like to know where all the exits are."

"Like a gunfighter in a saloon."

"Exactly."

"How'd you know where to find me?" she asked him again.

"You told me."

"I haven't even seen you in years, Jack. I made this plan days ago."

"Pillow talk. Is that what they call it? Lying in bed all sweaty from phenomenal sex, telling the gorgeous babe with her head on your chest about your dream escape plan. And then listening while she tells you hers. That's pillow talk, right?"

"You're such an ass. Do you know what year it is? You don't get to talk to me like that anymore."

"I'm trying to turn you on."

"You're failing." He wasn't. She was remembering that night, just like he'd intended her to. "As I recall, you said—"

"When it all goes to hell, as it inevitably will," Jack filled in. "I'll cash in my wad and head to a tropical island. My own version of Margaritaville. Flip flops and salt in my beer."

It was easy to avoid looking at him. She just focused on driving and tried to pretend he wasn't there.

"And you said your paradise is a little place in New Mexico, in a village outside Taos, near one of those old churches where miracles happened. Our Lady of something or other."

She closed her eyes briefly. "I did tell you that, didn't I?"

"You did."

"And you remembered. All this time."

"I've got a good memory."

She nodded, looked at the mirror, frowned.

"What?" Jack turned in his seat to look behind them. There was a jacked-up pickup back there. "Is that one of them?"

"I don't know. Came from that last on-ramp. How the hell would he know where we were? He didn't follow us."

"He didn't follow us." Jack said. "Let's just see if it's him first, before we freak out."

"I'll get off the next—"

"No," Jack said, shaking a wrinkle out of his map and holding it over the dash. "There's nothing there. And no re-entry. Take the next exit after that. Connects to three possible escape routes."

She gave him a nod. "Nice."

"Yeah. Old stuff can still work pretty damn well. Keep that in mind."

"Jason, this is your mother's place."

"Yeah." Jason hit the button on his keyring, and the elegant gates that looked like antique white iron moved as if weightless. He drove through, and hit the button again, closing the gates behind them.

"Eve is expecting us to join her at Jack's hunting cabin. My

143

God, she's heading to some isolated shack to lead a killer away from me, and her only backup is Jack Kellogg."

"Call her." He handed her his phone, since she hadn't brought her own. "Tell her to come here instead. It's safer."

"Then why didn't you tell her where you were really going to begin with?"

"Because I didn't plan this. It was...spontaneous. And because this way, we get a few hours alone. And maybe you can relax a little, and give yourself time to catch up with what's happening to you."

"I'm not gonna relax."

"Yes, you are. Call Eve."

She rolled her eyes. "I don't have her number."

"Call Jack, then."

She got out of the truck, scrolled to the listing for Jack, tapped it and waited. "Why did you bring us here?"

"It felt like the right move. Mom and Ted are on a cruise, and—"

Eve picked up. "Jack's phone. Talk to me."

"It's me," Sunny said. "Jason pulled a fast one, drove us to his mother's place. He says you should come, too. Says it's safer here."

"He's trying to hold on," Eve said.

"To his family home?"

"To you, Einstein."

"Oh."

Jason was keying in a code and opening the front door. The place was opulent. It had a foyer like a hotel lobby, split staircases curving off in opposite directions, crystal chandelier the focal point.

"I don't think that's it," she said.

"Yeah, well, we can't come right now. Your brother is tracking us and we need to figure out how."

"What? Eve, no. You're not safe."

"We're fine. We've got a plan and I've got the whole FBI to back me up. I'm safe. Stay in touch."

"I'll text you the address here."

"Okay."

She hung up the phone and turned to Jason. "Braxton's guys are following them. They think they're tracking them somehow. They have a plan, but didn't say what. God, I hope Eve's okay."

"She seems extremely competent."

"Yeah. She's kickass. Saved my life once. More than once, but once in true kickass fashion."

"I would love to hear that story."

She tensed. He saw it. "I didn't mean now."

"Sorry. I just...I've been in the past enough for one day. I can't—"

"I get it. Tell you what, I'm going to see what I can find us to eat."

"Okay if I take a shower while you do that?"

"Entirely okay. You can relax, Sunny. You're safe here. And if I have my way on this, you'll be safe back home in Big Falls, too."

"You gonna fix my life for me, Jason?"

"You fixed it for yourself. I want to help keep your brother from wrecking it. If you don't mind."

"I don't mind." She paused, then said, "But you and me—"

"You're family, Sunny, regardless of you and me. It's not even about you and me right now. You're part of my family. You're a part of Big Falls. I don't think you even know how much. Let me help."

She took a breath, lowered her head. "I'll let you know."

She headed upstairs. Jason's mother kept one guestroom just for her, so she'd have her own space when they came to visit together. She'd been to three Thanksgivings here, and three with the Big Falls branch of Jason's family. Same with Christmases. They took turns.

But that was before. That was when she'd been sweet Sunny Cantrell.

The guest room had gradually transformed into a reflection of her. Jason's mother, Judith, had it re-painted pale sky blue with white curtains that billowed when the windows were open. Whenever Sunny came to visit, she'd find dresses and nightgowns in her size hanging in her closets. Or sometimes a drawer full of fluffy socks, or a new robe with matching plush slippers. Every time Liz discovered a beauty product she loved, she bought an extra one for Sunny, and left it for her to find in the attached bathroom.

She wanted Sunny for a daughter-in-law. What would she think of her when she knew the truth?

Sighing, she sat down at the vanity and looked at her reflection in the mirror. She didn't look like sweet Sunny Cantrell tonight. Her eyes were haunted, her hair as wild as her emotions, and you could see the bandage and dark edges of the tattoo even though she'd combed her blond hair over it. She was dressed for fight or flight. There was a bruise on her cheek. She'd banged it while diving out of the path of her brother's knife.

He wanted her dead. He'd have killed her if it hadn't been for Jason.

She looked into the mirror. She was not the angry, rebellious, terrified kid she'd been before. She was scared now in a grown-up way. It wasn't hidden. She could show it. She felt no shame in it. When someone's chasing you with a knife, intent on driving it into your heart, you're scared. It makes sense. So yes, she was scared. But she wasn't going to let it rule her.

She wasn't the Sunny she'd been pretending to be for the past six years either. She'd locked up her dark feelings so thoroughly it had been easy to forget their existence. She'd been happy, upbeat, friendly, kind, generous for six years. She'd rarely used a cuss word or lost her temper with anyone in all that time. She hadn't had a bad dream. She hadn't entertained a single hateful or murderous thought.

But that had been a lie, too. She'd grown up with hate. She'd witnessed murder. She'd hated, and she'd wished death on others. She'd lied, and she'd broken the law, and she'd supported and enabled an evil man. Her father.

Her entire time in Big Falls, she'd felt like the devil's daughter, posing as an angel on Heaven's country Main Street.

Honestly, she didn't know who she was now. Not Jillian, who Eve wanted her to become, that was for sure. She was pretty sure she never would be. Jillian and New Mexico were for someone else. Not her.

But was she Sunny Cantrell? Or was she Mary Sunlight Hayes?

She didn't feel like either one of them. She felt untethered from either identity, adrift in a sea of danger and potential.

❧

"That smells like Del Vecchio's." She'd come downstairs at last, all pretty in pink pajama bottoms with a matching tank, a lightweight lilac robe that looked like satin hanging loose and short. She wore pink ballet slippers made of fleece.

He was staring. She saw him staring. He saw her see it. The lights were all off, the big TV screen blue and blank. "It *is* Del Vecchio's. Sausage and mushrooms, your favorite. And Miller beer in Mom's frosted mugs."

"I love your mother's frosted mugs."

"Everybody loves my mother's frosted mugs." He waved a hand, and she followed it to the sofa. A soft blanket was draped over the back. He sat down beside her, aimed the remote and tapped a button. The movie started.

"Young Frankenstein," she said. "My favorite pizza, beer and movie. It's a trifecta."

"See? You're still you, Sunny. All the crap going on in your head is gonna take some sorting out, I know that, but you are still Sunny. I know you."

She sank onto the sofa beside him. They did this sometimes, when they were here visiting his mom, crept up in the middle of the night to commandeer the biggest screen in the place, always accompanied by junk food and beer.

He leaned forward to pull out a cheesy slice, and handed it to her with a napkin. "Let it go for a little while. Focus on the movie. You're safe here. Mom's got a great security system and the cops response time is only six minutes. You're safe."

He watched her try to do that, and after a while, he thought she'd succeeded. She was even laughing, after a while, and they did a good job depleting the pizza and the beer. By the time Madeline Kahn was belting out "glory hallelujah," she seemed much more like herself again. He put his arm around her. She didn't pull away. Instead she leaned her head on his shoulder. "I'm sorry I kept so much from you," she said.

"I'm sorry I let you."

"You didn't know—"

"Yeah, I did. I've been thinking about this, and yes. I knew there was something. And I know now why you kept it from me. The last guy you were involved with died because of your family. I wish you'd told me, but I understand why you didn't. And I think I know how hard it must've been to keep this to yourself all this time."

He tipped her chin up, looked into her eyes. "I want to take you back home in the morning. Back to Big Falls. We'll figure out the rest from there."

"If I go back, he'll come, too. It will put everyone at risk, Jason. Even Matilda Louise and Diana. All of them.

"We have support there. We have family there."

"You have family there."

"You still don't get how valued you are, do you?" He heaved a big sigh. "Just think about it, okay? He sets foot in Big Falls, Jimmy will arrest him. Don't give up your life for this jerk, Sunny. Stand and fight for what you care about. And for God's sake, for *our* sake, let me stand and fight beside you."

When she didn't say anything for a long time. He said, "Think about it while I teach you some moves."

She blinked at him.

"Come on, get up."

She got up slow. "You think I don't have moves?"

"You didn't have any back at the motel."

"I was freaked out. I have moves. I've been to the self-defense classes at the dojo."

"Well, then, let's see 'em."

"After three beers? I might hurt you." They moved into the expanse of carpet between the coffee table and the TV. "I might hurt myself."

He smiled as he watched Sunny take up a crouching stance. She said, "Bring it on, big guy."

He lunged at her, and she dodged him. He grabbed her from behind, and she flipped him. He lay on his back on the floor, looking up at her. She put her foot on his chest and raised her fists in victory, so he grabbed her ankle and swept it right out from under her. She landed flat on top of him, face to face, and they were both laughing, until they weren't.

Her hair was hanging down like a curtain. He wanted to kiss her. But it had to be her idea. So he just held her eyes, and pushed her hair behind her ear on one side.

"I wish none of this had happened."

"I'm not so sure I agree," he said.

"How can you say that?"

"Because I never would've got to know all of you, the way I'm doing now."

"The parts I kept from you are parts I'm ashamed of."

"I don't mean the events. Most of which weren't in your control anyway. No, I mean you. Mary Sunlight Hayes Cantrell."

She seemed to just take that in for a second.

"Never say I don't know you again. I do know you. You've been trying to figure out who you are. Sunny or Mary."

"I have."

"Has it hit you yet that you're both? And you're kind of kick-ass under all that sparkle."

She flopped off him, onto her back, a forearm landing across her brow. "How can I be both? They're opposites."

"They're you," he said. "No one's all light, Sunny. Our dark corners are what give us depth. Our shadows make us 3D. I feel like I'm seeing the whole you for the first time."

"Yet, you're still here," she said, heavy on the sarcasm.

"Yeah. I'm still here. It's good, that you noticed that."

She lowered her forearm and rolled up onto one side. "Are you...trying to say we might not be over?"

"I'm trying to say you never had to hide yourself from me, and you don't have to now, Sunny. So, if there are any more secrets, any more lies—"

"Stories. Pieces of the past. But no more secrets. You know everything now."

He shrugged. "And again, I'm still here."

She stared into his eyes and hers grew shiny. And then she leaned closer, and pressed her mouth to his. He wrapped her up in his arms, snugged her body tight, kissed her like his life depended on it. He got up slowly, gathering her with him, up to his knees and then onto his feet, and he carried her across the room, and up the stairs, still kissing her.

"How is a night in a fancy hotel going to shake off those creeps who've been following us?" Eve asked.

"Just keep the coat over the cat carrier, and smile." Jack sauntered up to the front desk like he was the king of Siam. "I phoned ahead," he told the clerk, though he hadn't. "My beloved needs to get to our room immediately, please. She's exhausted."

"Of course, of course! Mister, er—"

He slapped a black card onto the desk, and said, "Please, hurry."

The clerk hit a bell and said, "Take this guest to the Coltry Suite."

A bellman rushed to Eve, reaching for the coat-covered cat carrier. She dodged and said, "I carry my own bag. Just give me the key and point me in the right direction." She did not even try to sound like the Queen of Sheba.

He handed her the key. "Take the elevator to three, then go left. It's the corner suite."

"Nice. I wonder who's paying for it." She glared at Jack and took the elevator up, then went down the hall and let herself in.

The room was *nice*.

She did a trust fall onto the bed let her bones relax for a few minutes. And then a few more. She didn't even move. She started to nod off, even, but then

Jack popped into the room.

"Okay, perfect, perfect. We left everything in the car..."

"Except the cat."

"The concierge is filling our list as we speak. New clothes right to the skivvies, two dispose-a-phones. New cat carrier. Something chi-chi. That cat's unhappy in there."

"She has to get out," Eve said, looking at the cat carrier beside her on the bed. Griselda was curled up and napping.

"There's a patio and a potted plant on the balcony," Jack suggested.

"She'll get away. Sunny'll kill us both."

"Well she can't stay in the carrier longer." He opened the carrier door. Griz lifted her head, then came out deliberately, not hurrying, jumped off the bed, and proceeded to inspect the premises.

"There's a bag of litter and a small box in the car," Eve said.

"You brought kitty litter while running for your life?"

"I knew we might be running for our lives when I got to Big Fall. I also knew she had a cat. I like to be ready for anything."

"I remember that about you."

"I'll go get it," she said.

"No, no. Let me. You're wiped out. But let's not get anything else from the car. We'll order up a rental, have it delivered. Then in the wee hours, we get in it with our new cat carrier, our new clothes, our new phones, and not one damn thing that was in the other car."

"Track *that,* jack-asses," Eve said.

Jack left the room to get the things for Griselda. Griz was exploring the room, probably looking for the facilities. "Hey, kitty. You must be hungry, huh. Good thing for you I thought to grab a can of cat food from the crateful your human made me put in the back of my car when we packed up the place."

Griz sent her a hateful look, turned around and walked under the bed.

Eve took the can from her small bag and popped the top.

The cat shot out from under the bed as if something in there had bitten her, stopping right at Eve's feet. She reached up with a paw, swiping at the can as Eve set it on the floor. "Sorry there's no pretty dish."

Jack returned in record time. He'd carried the litter and litter box up in a suitcase he must've emptied in the car. "Where do you think? Bathroom?"

"That's what it's for."

So, he carried it in, and she heard him open the bag and pour the litter. Then he turned on the fan to get rid of the dust, and came back out. "Problem solved."

They watched the cat eat every molecule of cat food. She

licked the can for a full minute after the food was all gone, then walked right into the bathroom. Eve picked up the can and followed to rinse it, fill it and with water. She set the water on the floor. Griz sniffed it then drank her fill, before going to check out the new box.

"Now what?" she asked. "I mean, I should update my boss, but other than that–"

"Update your boss without mentioning my name. Other than that, there's nothing else we need to do right now. We can enjoy the room. Watch a movie, order some room service, hit that mini bar."

"Whose black card are you using, Jack?"

"What are you talking about?"

"I saw the card. Jet black. Only movie stars and billionaires have those. Not two-bit grandpa con-artists."

"I was never a two-bit con artist, and you know it. I was an amazing con-artist. And I'll have you know I'm also a top-notch grandpa."

"No shit," she said, looking at him.

He pulled out his phone, scrolled to baby pictures. Him-holding-a-baby pictures. Him hugging his daughters, one in each arm, and another one with all of them, and the baby, too.

"Have you actually been tamed, Jack Kellogg?"

"Never. I'm just keeping it legal. It's what my girls want, and hell, I was ready to retire anyway. You want the first shower?"

Aha, he didn't want to talk about his former career, or its end. Alleged end. "Yeah," she said, cutting him a break since he was helping her.

"Good. And then we'll eat and get some sleep. We skip this joint at three a.m."

She nodded. "You're very good at deception."

"Thank you for the compliment."

"It wasn't a–"

There was a tap on the door, and Jack said, "There's the kid now. And within the hour I gave him. You might as well wait for fresh clothes."

Eve leaned in the bathroom doorway and watched him greet the employee, compliment him on his speed, and sign away what must've been a generous tip. The way the kid's eyes lit up.

"Thank you, sir. Anything else you need, you call downstairs and ask for Ronny."

"I'll do that. How long is your shift Ronny?"

"I'm pulling a double. I'll be here 'til six a.m."

"That's great. I'll have something for you later. Listen, now we need to be real clear on this. Did anyone ask about these errands, what you were getting or who you were getting it for?"

"No sir. Only Eric—the Concierge—knows, and he's the most tight-lipped guy you ever saw."

"Good. And how about you? Are you tight lipped?"

"You can trust me, sir."

"I'll double that tip if you get me a rental car, and have it here before three a.m. I want you to slip it into the hotel garage so casually that nobody gives it a second look."

He nodded. "I can do that. People arrive in the middle of the night all the time."

"That's perfect, Ronny."

"You guys...like, under cover or something?"

"Or something. Not a word, or no giant tip."

"Yessir!"

Jack took the bags, including a pair of garment bags, and tossed them onto the bed. There was only one, but the small sofa folded out. Jimmy left, whistling as he pulled the door closed behind him.

"He's gonna talk," Eve said.

"Not 'til after he gets that tip, though. Human nature. If I'd paid up front, he'd already be texting his girlfriend about it." He unzipped the garment bags, taking a little red dress out of hers.

"You better have had him buy the jeans I asked for." She went

154

to the bed, dug through the bags, found the one with her requested undergarments, jeans, tank top, and green cargo jacket. She picked up the socks and a pair of little black boots with silver buckles. "Damn, the boy can pick footwear. These are cute."

"And on a deadline, no less."

. She took her stuff and went into the bathroom. When she took off her clothes, she wrapped them in the store bags and tied them in knots. Nothing from her car was going with them. Braxton Hayes must have planted a tracker somewhere. It was probably on the car itself, but it could be anywhere, tucked away in the lining of a bag or the pocket of a jacket or in anything else they'd brought with them.

So, they'd leave it all behind.

"Let's head down to Jason's from here," she called through the closed door. "I don't like that Sunny's so far away. Anything could happen."

"Fine by me. Long as we can order room service in the meantime."

CHAPTER 14

"So after you helped them convict your father, you went into witness protection?"

She was lying across Jason's chest. He'd driven every worry and fear from her mind for a little while, but now they were all clamoring at the doorways of her mind. "Yeah."

"And you became Sunny Cantrell."

"Eve said I should think about the woman I wanted to be. She said most people don't get a chance to start over. I thought about the woman I imagined my mother was. I didn't know much about her—I was only three when she died. My memories of her are thin and hazy, but there was that photo. I took it when I left for college. She was wearing that pale blue dress, and a little white cardigan with pearl buttons. And her hair was blond as summer sunshine. And I remembered how she used to call me Mary Sunlight. That's my clearest memory of her, really. She's holding me and twirling in circles outside and singing 'Pretty Mary Sunlight, she's all right with me'." She sang a few lines, the way she remembered them.

"I told Eve the next day that I wanted to keep Sunshine as a part of my name to remind me of my mother. My father hated that name, always blamed it on her, said she filled in the name on her own in the hospital after she had me. Never consulted him, he said. He hated that my middle name was Sunshine. I loved it because my mother gave it to me. I wanted to be a baker like she was, too. I'd heard Dad say she could bake the angels right off the clouds."

"So can you," he said, stroking her hair.

"I don't know how Eve made it happen, but she did. I became Sunny Cantrell, and I had a job working at the Big Falls Bakery for Miss Sarah Jane Olson."

"That's kind of a beautiful story," he said.

"It didn't feel like it to me. I felt like such a fraud. I thought everyone who walked into the bakery knew for sure I wasn't who I was pretending to be. And then I just realized one day I wasn't pretending anymore."

"You just let her out, that's all. She was always inside you."

She thought about that, about how hard she'd tried to be a good little girl, to please her father, to take care of the family the way she imagined her mom would've done. Had she been Sunny then?

"And then," he prompted.

"Aren't you sleepy?"

"I am. Are you?"

"Getting there."

"So talk 'til you're sleepy."

She breathed deep. "One day Miss Sarah told me she wanted to retire and sell the bakery, and that she thought I could make a go of it. She offered it to me, owner-financed at a monthly payment she knew I'd be able to afford. And then, when she passed away last year, she left me the title free and clear."

"How can you think about leaving all that behind?"

She had declared her life worth fighting to keep in front of him. But she wasn't sure if she had the courage to see that through. Facing her brother instead of running from him? People died last time she'd tried to stand against her family.

~

Sunny kept drifting off, then coming awake with a start. Every time she slept, she relived the parts of her story that Jason still didn't know.

Every time she closed her eyes, her brother's men were holding her down while Braxton tattooed the hate symbol on her head. He was rough, pushing hard, drilling the ink deep and dragging the needle so fast it pulled and tore the already raw skin. It hurt. It bled. She was terrified.

"We're gonna kill you, little Sis. I just want you to know that while the rest of this goes down. You need to be punished. You need to suffer for what you did. And the whole time you're suffering, I want you to know it only ends when I say it ends, and when I do, you die. But that's gonna be a long time from now."

One of the guys came into her sight. He had jumper cables. They ran back to the car and were attached to its battery terminals. He tapped the toothed clamps together and they shots sparks.

"Our father murdered innocent people, Braxton."

"Nobody's innocent." He looked up suddenly, like he'd heard something. "Watch her." He went to the small door in the back of the place, looking out each window he passed on the way. Then he opened the back door and ducked through it, and closed it behind him just as the front door exploded inward.

Eve leaped through like some kind of super hero, guns blazing. She didn't say freeze, she didn't say anything. She shot both of Brax's lackeys and led Mary out of that garage while they lay writhing on the floor, begging for their lives. Police and an ambulance came fast, but Brax got away. Mary Sunlight Hayes vanished from the face of the earth that night.

And Sunny Cantrell was born before the next morning.

But Mary hadn't died. She was awake and clawing her way out of the basement where she'd been locked up all these years. Sunny felt her anger; she felt her outrage. How dare her father kill Dave? How dare her brother blame her for her father's death. How dare he drive her out of a life she loved?

They couldn't both live on this planet, Mary said. She'd been saying it for a long, long time now, but Sunny hadn't been listening. She hadn't needed to listen. She'd had a perfect life, and Braxton hadn't found her. She'd been going through her days as if that would always be the case.

But Mary had known the whole time. She'd always known. One of them had to die.

The doorbell rang, echoing Big Ben's chime sequence through the house. Sunny sat up fast, flung back the covers.

"It's fine, I've got this," Jason said, and he had his pants on and headed downstairs while she was still wrestling into her pink pajamas. She stepped into the slippers on her way past them and went into the hall and down the curving staircase to the foyer. Jason was standing near the door, talking into a panel on the wall. "I'm opening the gate," he said.

"What's going on?"

"Eve and Jack are out front. They shook whoever was following them and came to join us here."

"Oh. Good."

"Really?"

She shrugged. "Why not?"

"I don't know. I'd hoped for a little more time alone with you, to be honest. At least breakfast." He smiled and kissed her head, then opened the front door.

Eve came in first, Jack right behind her with a hot pink cat carrier Sunny had never seen before. "Aw, Griz. There you are. I missed you!" Sunny opened the carrier and pulled her cat into her arms, despite Griselda's growling protests.

"We're fine, thanks. And you?" Eve said, while looking around and nodding. "Damn, this is like a resort. How long do we get to stay?"

"What happened to my cat's old carrier?"

"We ditched it," Jack said.

Eve nodded. "And the car, and our clothes, and our phones, and everything else we brought from Big Falls. They were tracking us."

"But we outsmarted 'em." Jack said with a wink. "Got a hotel, left everything there, and sneaked off in a rental car wearing brand new duds. So what's to eat around here?"

"Griz is asking the same thing, I think." Sunny was trying to keep Griselda from twisting free, but it was a losing battle.

"You can put her down," Jason said. "Griz has been here before, she knows her way around."

"I'll show her again, just in case." Sunny carried the cat out of the room, through the kitchen to the small utility bathroom no one used. The washer and dryer lived there, along with a big deep sink and racks of cleaning products. The spotless, covered, self-scooping litter box was in the corner. There was an elaborate cat tower in front of the room's only window. Griz ran to it as soon as Sunny put her down. She sniffed delicately before hopping her way to the middle platform where she could bat a dangling catnip bird while lying down.

She was happy. For the moment.

There was an array of kitty dishes on a top shelf, and in the cabinet above it, a year's supply of canned cat food in various flavors.

She found a can and a pair of stainless-steel bowls, which she promptly filled.

Griz dove off the tower and dug in like she was starving. Poor cat. Sunny scratched her head, but she growled. She did not like being touched while she was eating. "Fine, be solitary. Come find me when you're done." Griz glanced up at her, licking her lips, and saying *Go away. I vant to be alone*, with her eyes. The standoffish feline had probably had enough of humans for one day.

She headed out of the laundry room, and followed voices down the hall toward the kitchen.

"Braxton is more sophisticated than he was last time I had to deal with him," Eve was saying. "A GPS isn't anything I'd have credited him with having the brain power to think of. Much less planting one where I couldn't find it."

"You couldn't use like…a sweeping device?" Jason asked.

"Sure, if I had one in my back pocket."

Jack said, "We should've let him catch up, and given the local law a heads-up."

Eve looked at him like he'd lost his mind. "And then what?"

"We induce him to commit a crime," Jack said. "Like, I don't know assaulting a McIntyre? Or maybe a federal agent?"

Eve tilted her head to one side. "I notice you're not suggesting we let him pound on *your* pretty face, Jack."

"Well, no. Assaulting an ex-con isn't gonna carry any weight."

Sunny said, "I know you guys are all wound up, but I'd really like to get a few more hours of sleep before sunrise."

"Yeah, us too," Eve said.

Jason said, "Me three. When you guys finish your snack, go upstairs, turn right, and pick any rooms that are unlocked."

"His mother keeps them all stocked with new toothbrushes and bath stuff for guests," Sunny said. "It's like coming to a hotel, only better. You should check out the pool if you're here long enough."

Jack clapped his hands. "Oh, *hell* yeah. But where are the butlers and maids and ass wipers?"

Jason rolled his eyes and left with Sunny. He stopped outside his bedroom door. "Is it wrong that I'm nervous letting Jack roam around my mom's place unsupervised?"

"It would be wrong not to," she said. "But he's a con man, not a thief. And Eve is keeping a good eye on him. An awfully close eye on him, actually." She frowned, wondering what that was about.

"Mom's good silver comes up missing, she'll shoot me." He smiled at her. "We're gonna figure this out. Things'll look better in the morning."

"I bet they will."

They stood there awkwardly for a moment. Then he blurted, "I hired Riley Everett to investigate your background."

She was so stunned she couldn't answer right away. It took her a beat. "You had me investigated by my best friend's sister-in-law?"

"Ex-sister-in-law. And yes, I did. So, I knew about your father. Just the headlines though. I didn't know you were the reason he was convicted, or that the man he killed was your first love. And I'm real sorry, Sunny. Sorry it happened, and sorry I didn't just wait for you to tell me yourself. I thought you were in danger. I thought I could help."

"Well, I was. And you have. And I suppose hiring Riley was better than hiring your sister Melusine."

"Step-sister, and you're right. Mel wouldn't have been as objective."

"I love that about your family."

"They're your family, too." He shrugged one shoulder. "You know, if you want 'em. Anyway, I'm gonna take a shower. If you still want to stay with me tonight–"

"I do."

"You're not mad?"

163

She shook her head. "How big a hypocrite would I have to be, to be mad?" She stood on tiptoe, kissed him softly. "Take your shower. I'm gonna go downstairs, see if I can coax Griz to come up here with us. I've missed her."

"I've missed her, too, but don't tell her." He sent her a wink and went into the bedroom, straight through the bathroom, dropping trou on the way. He looked over his shoulder at her in all his bare-assed glory, winked, and then he closed the bathroom door.

She caught was smiling as she walked back to the stairway. She was actually feeling hopeful. Maybe her life as Sunny Cantrell really wasn't over. Then again, not everyone in Big Falls was going to be as understanding as Jason was. Even if she could escape her brother's wrath once and for all, the community might never accept her again. They were upright people.

She thought about how everyone secretly mistrusted Jack Kellogg, because he'd done time. And conned the town out of millions once. But Kiley got it back for them. She didn't want to be looked at the way Jack was. She couldn't run a business if people thought she was a racist like her father and her brother.

She wandered through the ground floor, calling "Hey, Griz. Where are you kitty?"

A soft meow floated from the back of the house, so she headed that way. Griz sat at the big glass patio doors, swiping her paw over the glass. Beyond them a curving flagstone patio stretched out all the way to the pool.

"Ah, honey, I'm afraid you'll get lost if I let you out." She went to the glass doors and picked up her cat. She heard laughter, noticed the pool lights were on and Jack and Eve were splashing around in the water.

Seeing Eve so relaxed made Sunny realize she'd been relaxing too. Braxton didn't know where Jason's mother lived. He'd have no reason to come here, and no way to follow them.

Not with the precautions Jack and Eve had taken. She stroked her cat, holding her in one arm.

"We're really safe, aren't we, Griz?"

Griz brought a hind leg forward and started digging at her collar. "Whoa, whoa, hey, easy now." She stopped her from scratching herself, then frowned at the spot she'd been digging, which was missing a little bit of fur. "Oh my poor kitty! You dug your hair out. What is going on with your collar?" She took hold of the pretty collar with its fake diamond studs, found the buckle, and undid it. Griselda twisted out of her arms and jumped to the floor. She shook her head rapidly, happy to have the thing off, Sunny surmised. She turned the collar over to see what was irritating her, and spotted it right away. It was a little round electronic button.

A loud crash came from out front, then a roaring motor, and before she could even react, the nose of a full-sized SUV smashed right through the patio doors. Glass exploded and she scrambled backward raising her arms over her face, tripping and falling on her ass.

Two guys got out, grabbed her wrists and dragged her through the broken glass. They shoved her into the front seat. Eve was shouting and racing toward them as the vehicle lurched backward, then surged around the house to the front.

"How's the rich boy's fancy-ass security doing now, Mary Sunlight?"

It was the same guy. It was the same guy who'd held her down while her brother tattooed her head. There'd been Landry Mason and Major. Eve should've shot to kill back then, rather than leaving them wounded on the floor of that abandoned garage where they'd taken her. They were already bounding over the smashed-in gate and onto the road. Jason came racing out the front door, barefoot and shirtless, but it was too late.

She was bouncing right off the seat as they sped away.

"Come back here with me, sis." It was Braxton. He was in the back. There were no seats back there. They were either folded down or had been removed. "It's time to pay for your crimes. Come on back, sis. Don't make me stab you through the nice upholstery."

"Not in the truck, dude," the driver said. "You promised."

"Then lose the damn cavalry so we can take her *out* of the truck."

Cavalry? She looked at the side mirrors. Jason's truck was speeding behind them. Eve's rental car was doing its best to keep up.

"Never mind. I'll do it myself." Brax slid his hunting knife into its sheath on his hip, and rolled onto his belly. There was a rifle on his back, its strap around his shoulder. He crawled toward two upright rear doors that opened in the center, and he flung them wide.

"No!" Sunny scrambled over the console into the back as the other two tried to stop her.

He pulled the rifle around and started shooting. Eve's car windshield exploded, and the car went skidding wildly.

"No!" Sunny shouted again. She kicked free of the hands trying to hold her, and jumped onto her brother's back, wrapped her hands around the gun barrel and yanked with all she had. It was hot and it burned her hands. He rolled up and smashed her body into the side of the truck, but she didn't let go. She brought her knee up between his legs from behind. He grunted, let go of the rifle, and flipped around to punch her in the face, but she still wouldn't let go of the rifle and let him kill Jason. He'd have to kill her first.

He squeezed the trigger, each tiny explosion eardrum-shattering. And yet, she didn't let go. Bullets riddled the inside of the vehicle as they wrestled for the gun. The driver lurched forward and blood spattered onto the windshield in front of him. The SUV went out of control. Braxton let go of the rifle and she fell backward, she'd been pulling so hard. The weapon sailed out the back, as her brother dove over the seat to grab the steering wheel. The SUV careened, but she was free, and made a split-second choice to dive out the open back doors.

She hit the pavement and rolled several times, but she saw it all the same. The jacked-up SUV shot off the road and into space, its motor roaring, its horn blaring. And then there were crashing, smashing sounds followed by a splash.

After that, time seemed to slow. She knew Jason's truck had skidded to a stop nearby, that Jason was there. Eve and Jack, too. She closed her eyes, opened them again, and took a painful breath.

"Sunny!" Jason was beside her, touching her face, moving her hair. "Are you okay? How bad are you hurt?"

"Is he dead?" she asked.

"Can you sit up?"

She used Jason's forearms to pull herself to her feet, then limped to where the truck had gone over. There were pieces of it all the way down the steep, rocky drop-off, and a lake at the bottom. Her brother's ride sank deeper, an explosion of bubbles erupting in its wake. She didn't see any bodies, though.

Eve came to stand on her left, because Jason was on her right, all but holding her erect. "Is he dead?" she asked again.

"No one could've survived that," Jason said.

"We'll get divers in there, recover the bodies," Eve was already pulling out her phone. "I still don't know how the hell he knew where we were."

Sunny couldn't take her eyes off the surface of the water. Every part of her was tensed and waiting for Braxton to break the surface, roaring in outrage. "It was Griz's collar. There was a little device glued to it. I found it just before—are you sure he's dead, Eve?"

"The *collar*," she said, like she should've known. Then, "Why don't you take Sunny home, Jason?"

"Not until I know he's dead. I have to know for sure."

"Hey." Eve got in front of her, breaking her line of sight to the lake. She had tiny cuts on her face. "He shot at you. Your car—are you all right?"

"Yeah, thanks to a certain ex-con who pushed my head down and took the wheel." She glanced behind her. Jack stood a few feet away, and he had more cuts on him than Eve did from the flying bits of windshield glass.

Jack gave a nod, but didn't say anything. He seemed shaken, but otherwise all right.

Eve smiled slightly at him, then returned her attention to Sunny. "I've got this. The FBI has got this. We know what we're doing. You standing here bleeding all over the road isn't helping anybody. Look at yourself, girl."

Sunny looked down. Her pink pajama bottoms were shredded, and where her skin showed though, it looked like it'd been run over a cheese grater. She was barefoot, and standing funny on one side, because it hurt to put weight on that ankle. The front of the jammie top had tar ground into it, two buttons missing, and the pocket had torn loose.

"She's right, Sunny." Jason put an arm around her like he knew she couldn't stand much longer. She'd only just realized it herself. He led her to a nearby boulder and helped her sit down. He had a first aid kit and she didn't know where he'd got it. His truck was sideways, near the side of the road, and Eve's car was off the road, in the brush. There were sirens in the distance. He started wiping the sore places on her face with pre-medicated pads from the kit, and it stung.

"It isn't gonna do any good staying here," he said. He ran his hands along her arms, then down her legs. "You're all scraped up. The medics will clean you up better."

"I'm not going to a hospital."

"You were limping."

"I don't think anything's broken." She unbent her knees, moved her feet around to show him, and tried not to wince when it hurt. "Nope, nothing's broken." "Let me take you home, Sunny."

"Yeah. Back to your mom's. I'll get a shower, clean clothes. I'll be fine."

"Yeah, and then to our *real* home."

She shot to her feet. "What if he follows? What if hurts your family? What if he hurts Big Falls?"

He made a face at her, lips pulling thin, brows bending deep. "You've lived there how long, now? Nobody can hurt Big Falls." He steered her around, started back toward his truck, standing cockeyed atop some impressive skid marks. "You've gotta have a little faith in your hometown, Sunny."

She twisted her head to look behind her, at Eve, on the phone, sounding professional and in command. Eve moved the phone away from her face. "My people are already in contact with the Big Falls PD."

"That would be cousin, Jimmy," Jack said.

"Step-brother-in-law," Jason said.

"Police Chief," Eve said. "He'll have backup."

"He won't need it, though." Jason looked Sunny right in the eyes. "He's gone, Sunny. He's out of your life. You're free of all that for the first time. You can go wherever you want now. So where do you want to go? In your heart, Sunny, where do you want to go?"

She closed her eyes to block the tears that bubbled up for no reason, and then saw the Cimarron rolling lazily past her Princess Pavilion. She smelled the dry Oklahoma air, and felt its powerful sun on her skin. "Home," she said. "Take me home, Jason."

CHAPTER 15

S unny leaned against the passenger door, with the window rolled down. Outside, Jason pumped gas and tapped his phone one-handed to access the dreaded family text loop. She'd given him the okay. There was no way around it. She had to face them all with the truth.

He read aloud as he tapped. "Bringing Sunny home and calling family meeting. Sophie, bring your bag. Meet at bakery in two hours."

He looked up from his phone. "Good?"

"She doesn't need to bring her bag."

He tapped send. *Swoosh.* And just as fast, replies started pinging. "Sophie says, 'if she's hurt, go to closest ER.'" He tapped out his reply, still reading. "Tried that. No go."

She reached out the window and took the phone from his hand. "I'm fine, nothing's broken." Send. "Watch the kids. Look out for Strangers."

Replies came through to that one so fast that the messages were speeding up the screen and the pinging sounds tripped over each other. She handed the phone back out to Jason. He shut it off and pocketed it, replaced the gasoline nozzle. "You

171

don't need to worry about them. Eve's already filled Jimmy in. Everyone's safe. They're watching for trouble."

"He has other followers. If Braxton's dead, they're gonna blame me for it just like he blamed me for our father dying in prison."

"Eve knows all of that, too. Relax Sunny." He got in and started driving again.

Sunny laid her head back and tried to close her eyes. Griz climbed into her lap, recognizing the signs she might get a massage. She'd been hiding under Jason's bed when they'd gone back to the house for her. God, what a mess, and it was all her fault. Jason made calls to the insurance company and his mom while she showered. He assured Sunny the place would be repaired before Judith even got back from her cruise, but that didn't make her feel any better.

She'd wrapped large sections of her arms and legs in ointment-soaked gauze and put on the loosest clothes she could find in her room there, a pair of flowy yoga pants and a soft jersey tee-shirt.

She tried to believe her brother was dead. She imagined the phone ringing, and hearing Eve on the other end saying, "We found his body." She waited for her heart to knot up, for her throat to tighten.

"Why don't I feel anything?" she asked.

Jason was driving, watching her and driving and not pushing her to talk, just giving her room to process everything that had happened. "You're not in pain?" he asked.

"Oh no, it hurts like the very devil. I mean for Braxton. He's my brother. I should care if he's dead. I should feel sad."

He took a couple beats, then said, "I don't think there's any such thing as what you should feel. There's only what you do feel. And it can't be right wrong, it's just what you feel."

She nodded slowly. "He's the one who put the tattoo on my head."

He sent her a stunned look.

"After our father was found guilty, Eve wanted me to go into protection. I didn't want to. Braxton was out on bail, and he grabbed me right off the street. Took me to a filthy garage and had his boys hold me down while he shaved my head with his hunting knife. And then he drilled that ink into my scalp. Would've killed me then, if not for Eve."

He swore softly, then reached across to cover her hand with his. "I'm sorry. Baby, I'm so sorry."

She shrugged. "I don't think it's over. I don't think he's dead."

She was quiet for a while. Every mile marker taking them closer to home was a bittersweet mix to her. She missed Big Falls so much. But she was out now. Everyone would know who she was. She couldn't pretend anymore. She couldn't hide behind the persona she'd created. She felt like the stains of her past showed as clearly as her scrapes and bruises.

"I don't think I belong there anymore," she whispered.

"Well, let's just see what Big Falls thinks about that."

As they neared the bakery, she saw that the sidewalk in front was littered with bright colors... Flowers! There were bouquets of them piled all over, with other things among them—candy boxes, cards. "Oh my gosh...look at that."

"You were missed." He pulled up along the curb, because the driveway was full of vehicles, most of them belonging to his family.

Sunny got out, wincing a little when her feet touched the ground. It hurt to move after so long sitting still.

Jason came around the truck. "You okay?"

"All good. I maintain, as I always have, that this truck is farther from the ground than necessary."

"If you're gonna keep getting yourself beat up all the time, I'll add a step for you."

It was dark outside. The little gas lamp replica street lights were all glowing, and so were a lot of upper windows. Most of the businesses had second floors. Some were used for offices, others for storage, but most of them were apartments, rented out or occupied by the business owners. Her friends, her colleagues. Her community. Some were looking out those windows. Some even waved.

She walked along the sidewalk to the bakery's entrance and knelt to pick up a bouquet of mums. "Look at all the flowers." There were roses and lilies and black-eyed Susans. Someone had arranged them to leave a path through their center to the front door.

Vidalia Brand McIntyre was holding it open. "I got Mouse to unlock it for us. I hope you don't mind." Then she opened her arms. "Welcome home, Sunny. Everything's gonna be all right now that you're back."

In spite of herself, Sunny walked right into those open arms, and let Jason's step-mom hug her. She was careful not to hug too tight or too long, and then drew her inside, where everyone else waited. Joey and Emily with Matilda Louise. Em was pouring coffee and Matilda was helping. Rob and Kiley were there, and Rob was holding baby Diana on his hip so Kiley could be next in line to hug her. Angie Wakeland was next. "We love you so much," she said in Sunny's ear.

Sophie peeled away from her handsome husband Darryl. Their son Max handed her little black medical bag to her, and nodded hello to Sunny.

"All right, everyone," Vidalia called out. "Get some coffee and find a perch!" Then in a lower voice to Sunny, "I made coffee here. If I overstepped, you can kick me later."

"Thank you, Vidalia. Coffee sounds good."

"Come on, Sunny." Sophie took her arm and led her toward

the back, wending their way through so many familiar faces. Vidalia's daughters, all five of them, were there, and most of her sons in law, too, and they all greeted her, touched her, hugged her as she passed.

"Sophie's gonna take Sunny in the back and check her over while Jason tells us what we need to know," Vidalia said.

"The whole town really needs to hear this, Jason," Sunny called back.

"That's why Jimmy's not here," Vidalia replied. "He called a meeting over at the town hall. Everyone turned out. Of course, they're curious." Then she nodded. "Go ahead, Jason."

Sophie went into the kitchen in the back of the building with Sophie, but she flipped down the doorstop to prop it open so she could hear better. She sat on a bench near the sink, and the doc opened her bag.

"Most of you have heard bits and pieces of this, but I need to put it together for you. Sunny feels you all have a right to know the truth. When she came here, it was to start a new life with a new name. She had helped convict her father of murdering her first love, a boy she met in college. He was the protestor who was killed eight years ago at Barrier Park."

A flurry of murmurs, exclamations, nods.

"Sunny's not Sunny?" Kiley asked.

"Sunny is Sunny, but her given name was Mary Sunlight Hayes. Her father died in prison, and her brother served his time, got out and came after her for vengeance. Jack heard about it and tried to warn her in time."

Kiley said, "Wait, wait, wait, my father knew about this?"

"Yes, and he tried to help. In fact, he stayed behind in Texas with Eve DuVall, the FBI agent who helped Sunny escape her brother and start over."

MAGGIE SHAYNE

"Eve was an FBI agent?" Angie asked.

"Help her do what?" Kiley was louder.

"Earlier today, Sunny's brother tried to kill her. He shot at Eve, and Jack might very well have saved her life. Sunny and Braxton struggled in the back of his SUV, and she jumped out the back just before it went over a cliff and into a lake. That's why she's all banged up."

Again, a surprised murmur rippled through the group. Vidalia said, "Someone needs to take him in hand, that's what."

"His body hasn't been found yet, though the two thugs helping him were both killed. Sunny's sure that if he survived, he'll come after her again."

Sunny slid off the stool as Sophie finished up. She limped into the main part of the place again. "Even if he is dead, his followers, these neo-Nazi idiots, might try to take revenge on me. Maybe on anyone who helps me. I don't know if my being here is safe for you. For the town."

"Ohhh, I hope they do come here. I'm dying to meet these guys," Kiley said, rubbing her hands.

Vidalia said, "Sunny, girl, haven't you been in our family–or this town–long enough to know how this works? You're where you belong, darlin'. We take care of our own around here."

Then to Jason, " She's all but dead on her feet. Why don't you go on upstairs and get some rest. Everyone else, let's join Jimmy and the locals over at the town hall."

"We love you, Sunny."

"Get some rest."

"Take care, Sunny."

Every person touched her as they slowly cleared out, and she kept choking up. Kiley stayed until last, and hugged her less gently than the rest. "Don't you ever run away from us like that again. You hear?"

"I hear."

She was so fierce, and so sweet looking with her strawberry

176

blond curls and smattering of freckles. "Did my father really do all that?"

"He really did," Sunny said. "And uh, there's something up with him and Eve. I think they have a history."

"Him and Eve?"

Sunny nodded.

"Eve, the FBI agent?"

Sunny nodded again.

"That's like saying a fox has a history with a hen, you realize that, right?"

"Didn't say I could explain it."

"Holy smokes. I guess it's true, there's no female he can't charm." She kissed Sunny's cheek. "Thanks for the info. Get some rest." Then she headed outside.

Jason, who'd stepped out, returned with the cat carrier and a yowling feline who knew she was home and wanted out. He put his arm around Sunny's shoulders. Ready to try to reclaim your life?

"That was way too easy," she said.

"Or maybe you were way too worried. Come on. Let's get you upstairs."

Jason watched her sleeping from the chair next to the bed. He'd like to be in there with her, but he wasn't gonna let down his guard until he knew for sure her brother was dead. The truth was, Braxton's body not being found scared the hell out of him. That man's mind was all twisted up. He guessed hate would do that to you.

Sunny was twitching again, and her breaths went short and quick. It had been happening every twenty minutes or so. He went to her, leaned over her. She startled awake before he had the chance to whisper to her that everything was okay. Her eyes were wide and frightened, until they met his. And then the breath just sighed out of her, and her tense body relaxed.

He didn't blame her for keeping the truth from him. It was a pretty awful truth to have to carry around, and he had no idea what that would be like. Or how he would handle having a devil-father who'd killed the one he loved. He didn't know how Sunny had come out of all that as well-adjusted as she was.

When he thought about what her brother had done to her, he was pretty sure he was capable of killing the guy himself. He didn't like thinking it. He'd have preferred to go through life not knowing that about himself.

He still loved her. There was a lot more to get to know about her, but he hadn't found anything he didn't love yet. He didn't think he was going to. But she'd been through so much, and she was still in shock, he thought.

She sucked in a breath and sat straight up.

He was still sitting on the edge of the bed, and he caught her shoulders, hands on autopilot. "It's okay. I'm right here."

She met his eyes and it happened again. The fear went away, she smiled with her eyes, and his heart melted.

She'd better want him back, because there wasn't gonna be another woman. Not after Sunny. Who could hold a candle?

She relaxed back down, snuggling into the pillows.

His phone rang and he grabbed it off the nightstand so it wouldn't wake her, and headed out of the room.

"Hey, it's Jack. How's it going there? How's Sunny?"

"Jack. It's good to hear your voice." Oddly, he thought, he meant that. Had he actually started to like the guy? "She's okay, physically at least. She's scared."

"I don't blame her. You see Kiley?"

"Yeah. I told her you were a hero."

"You didn't have to—"

"It's the truth, Jack. You helped. A lot, and there was no reason.—"

"What reason? I'm your brother's father-in-law. There oughtta be a word for that."

"Father-out-law," Jason said.

"Oh, you *must* be feeling better about things, making jokes that bad."

"Is there news, Jack?"

"Yeah. Big news. The guy you tried to eviscerate is awake, doing better, out of the ICU and in a regular room, cuffed to the bedrail with a guard on his door. A dozen members of his group are coming to bust him out, and word is, Braxton Hayes will be with them."

Ice rushed up Jason's spine, making him stand straighter. "He's alive."

"Yeah, according to what the feds picked up. I guess some of the group's more active members have been discussing their plan to take Landry Mason out of the hospital."

"They actually *heard* them say Hayes would be with them? Were they bugged or something?" He needed to know for sure. He couldn't tell Sunny her brother was alive if he didn't know for sure."

"Probably tapped into their smartphones from outer space or some modern shit. There's no privacy anymore. Anyway, they're heading for Tucker Lake General, heavily armed, tonight."

"My God, everyone in the hospital—"

"They'll never get inside. That's why I'm calling instead of Eve. She's with her people, setting up to ambush them. The hospital will be locked up tighter'n Fort Knox."

"Good. Good. When is all this happening?"

"Now. I mean, who knows when Brax'll show up, but the cops are already at Tucker Lake General. You didn't notice the mass exodus?"

"We've been kind of holed up here. Trying to let her rest."

"They called in everyone," Jack said. "Local PDs, state police, even the feds they sent out to back up Chief Jimmy. So you can tell Sunny not to worry. If her brother's alive, he'll be in a cell before the night's out. And this time he'll stay there."

"I hope you're right," Jason said. "Thanks, Jack."

"Eve told me to call and fill you in."

"Not for the call. For...everything. I mean it. Thank you."

It took him an extra second to reply, "You're welcome."

Sunny dreamed she was sleeping in her bed, and Braxton was standing over her, his face waterlogged, his hair dripping seaweed, turning his knife slowly in his hand, and deciding where to stab her first. In the dream, she woke up and saw him there, but she couldn't move. She tried to scream, but no sound would come out. He slid the blade slowly into her belly.

She woke with a lung-bursting gasp and sat up, pressing a hand to her chest. Her heart was racing. She couldn't catch her breath.

"Hey, hey, you're all right. I'm right here." Jason sat on the edge of the bed, held her shoulders softly, gazed into her eyes. And she could breathe again.

He was fully dressed. Deep down, he must not think Braxton was dead, either. If he did, he would be in bed with her. But he was up, watchful, protective. It was just his way. His family's way. They all looked out for each other.

They wanted to look out for her, too. They'd get hurt though.

She flung back the covers, and slid out the other side of the bed.

"You've only had a few hours of sleep," Jason said.

"The dreams are too bad. I can't close my eyes again." She frowned and said, "Did you get a call earlier?"

He nodded. "Yeah, it was Jack with an update. C'mon, I'll make us a sandwich. You've gotta be starved."

"What was the update?" She stayed still, standing beside her bed, her back toward her bedroom window and its view of the world's most perfect Main Street. Everything in her was tense, waiting for word that her brother was dead. For sure, finally, dead.

"They picked up some chatter, I guess. Some of your brother's guys are going to try to bust Landry out of the hospital tonight."

"And...?"

"There's a chance Braxton is going to be with them."

It was like everything warm drained from her body, right through the floor. She was made of ice. She could hardly move. "How did they..."

"Some of the guys are bugged or something. But it's all fine. The FBI and every cop in the area are converging on Tucker Lake General. If it was even true that he's with them, he'll be in custody before the night's out."

She closed her eyes slowly. "Dad and Brax always knew who was being surveilled. They'd play games, say things to send law enforcement on wild goose chases...or get them out of the way if they had something illegal planned."

A cold finger dragged itself up her spine as if a monster were standing behind here. She forced herself to turn around and look out the window.

Torches danced on Main Street, one of them painting her brother's battered, filthy face as red as the devil's.

He looked up, right at her window, and she ducked away, even though he couldn't possibly see her with the lights off in the room.

"Come on out, Mary!" He bellowed the words, and his voice was hoarse. He wasn't well. "Come on out and take what you're owed, or I swear on our father's name, we'll burn this whole damn town!"

They raised their torches, every one of them.

Jason had come and wrapped his arms around her, and she didn't know when. She heard him talking and realized he was on the phone. She didn't know who he was talking to. "It was a distraction. Braxton Hayes is here with twelve others, waving tiki torches and threatening to burn the town."

"He'll do it," Sunny said, and she heard the way her voice trembled. "I have to go–"

"Don't be–"

"I can't let them burn Big Falls!" She used Jason's self-defense lesson against him, swept his legs out from under him, and shoved his chest in the opposite direction. He went down like a redwood, and she bounded over the bed and out of the room, through the apartment to the stairs. Jason was right behind her, but she slammed the stair door and turned the deadbolt on the outside.

He'd have to take the outside stairs in back.

She ran through the bakery, where vases of flowers stood on every table, all the windowsills, and the front counter. Jason. He must have done that while she'd been sleeping.

Her heart twisted a little, but she didn't slow down. She lunged out the front door, her bare feet slapping onto the sidewalk. "Here, I'm here!" she cried.

Her brother had his hunting knife in his hand. Most of his cohorts had rifles, but he just had that stupid knife. She hated that knife. He took a step toward her.

Jason came barreling around the corner of the building.

"Hold it right there." One of the thugs dropped his torch and raised a shotgun, but Jason didn't stop, he kept coming, barreling toward her. There was a gunshot and she screamed.

Jason's arms came around her and his momentum carried them to the sidewalk beside his truck, parked at the curb.

"Who's next?" A woman shouted. Wait, was that *Vidalia's* voice?

"Drop your weapons, boys. You're completely surrounded." And that sounded like Joey.

Jason was getting up, helping her to her feet. He didn't seem to have any bullet holes in him. As weapons clattered on pavement, Sunny and Jason looked over the pickup bed at the unlikely scene unfolding on Main Street. Locals lined the sidewalk on the opposite side, and blocked both ends of the street, every one of them armed. The man who'd been about to shoot Jason was lying still in the road. His torch lay beside him, still burning. The others had dropped their weapons, and raised their hands and her brother cried, "Nooooo! No, she has to pay!"

She stood up straighter, looked him right in his eyes. "It's over, Brax. It's all over. You could've just left me alone. Now you're gonna die in prison like our father did."

"You're right. So what've I got to lose?" He reached behind him, brought a handgun around his body, pointed it at her. It was all happening in slow motion. She heard the explosion just as Jason pushed her hard. A dozen other shots went off, and she hit the sidewalk and so did he. He was bleeding!

Sunny scrambled to Jason's side. He was sitting up, hand clutching his upper arm, blood oozing between his fingers. "Jason's shot!" she shrieked, her eyes moving rapidly from his bleeding arm to his face.

"I'm okay. It went right through, it's barely a gash."

"Your whole damn family is here! Where the hell is Sophie?" She squeezed his arm up higher than the wound, and twisted her head around to see if help was coming.

And then she went still. Braxton lay in the road behind Jason's truck, right underneath the street lamp. It was like a spotlight. His body was riddled with bullet holes. He wasn't moving.

"I've got him, Sunny," Sophie said.

Sunny looked at her. She'd come along the sidewalk from somewhere. She had her bag. She knelt beside Jason, tearing his shirt sleeve open.

Sunny straightened to her full height, and walked slowly toward where Braxton lay. There was a lot of blood.

Jason's brothers, and brothers-in-law were marching thugs toward the police station, past Vidalia, who supervised the little parade with a double barrel shotgun almost as tall as she was. All Brax's boys had their hands bound behind them with zip ties, and all of them were looking backwards at where their leader lay.

Everyone else lingered. They'd broken into groups of three or five, talking soft and watching.

"Wyatt's gone to get the ambulance."

"Won't matter for that guy. Jeeze."

"How many of us you figure shot him anyway?"

"I did. You?"

"Twice."

She was standing over her brother now. The gun was in front of her feet, so she kicked it away. The knife was lying where he'd dropped it.

Finally, she looked at his face. And that's when she knew for sure he was gone. His eyes were open, just like Dave's had been. And just as lifeless.

Her throat tightened up so much it was hard to breathe. He'd been her baby brother once. She'd held him, and fed him, and played with him and loved him. He'd hated her, murdered her love, scarred her for life, and tried to kill her.

Tears fell. She let them.

CHAPTER 16

A week had gone by. She'd reopened the bakery. Main Street had been cleaned up, and Jason's truck was at the body shop, although his brother Joe opined that the bullet-holes made it look tougher.

She was waiting for Jason in the Princess Pavillion, relaxing in a cool breeze while the river rolled past. She heard his loaner car pull in and turned to see him come strolling down the path, wine bottle in one hand, fresh flowers in the other.

"That's nice," she said. "The others are wilting and I really love having fresh flowers in the place. Especially daisies."

He came up the steps, and she took the flowers as he swept her into his arms for a kiss. She held the flowers behind his head, he held the wine behind her back, and they kissed long and slow. That was the way they kissed hello and goodbye every time now. Just one of many tiny changes. They were more to each other now. Things were deeper between them now. Better.

When he stopped kissing her, he poured the pre-chilled wine. "No one else got you daisies," he said, handing her hers.

"No one else did," she said.

"I know they're your favorite. You're kind of nuts about daisies, actually."

"You know me so well," she said.

"Yes, I do. I have right along. Now, I know you even better." He downed the wine in a gulp, then said, "And damned if I'm not a glutton for punishment, but uh..." He pulled a little white box from his pocket, and dropped to one knee. "At least look at the ring this time before you shoot me down?" And he opened the box.

The ring winked up at her, a yellow diamond center surrounded by white diamond petals. "It's a daisy!"

"That it is. And we'll have them at our wedding. All the daisies the church will hold. I love you Sunny. I love your light, and I love your shadows. I love your laugh and I love your temper. I even love your arrogant, hostile cat. And that's not gonna change. So, I'm asking you to be my wife. All of you. Mary Sunlight Hayes Cantrell McIntyre."

She didn't answer. She looked at him there, on one knee proposing to her, the best man she'd ever known. Behind him the Cimarron was singing low, as the sun set far upstream.

"Sunny?"

She looked back at him, savoring every detail of the moment. And she smiled, and said, "Sunny McIntyre will do."

"That'll do just fine." He got up and put the ring on her finger.

"Perfect fit," she said.

"That's exactly what we are. A perfect fit." And he kissed her once more.

THE END

ALSO AVAILABLE

The McIntyre Men
Oklahoma Christmas Blues
Oklahoma Moonshine
Oklahoma Starshine
Shine On Oklahoma
Baby By Christmas
Oklahoma Sunshine

The Oklahoma Brands
The Brands who Came for Christmas
Brand-New Heartache
Secrets and Lies
A Mommy For Christmas
One Magic Summer
Sweet Vidalia Brand

ABOUT THE AUTHOR

New York Times and *USA Today* bestselling novelist Maggie Shayne has published sixty-two novels and twenty-two novellas for five major publishers over the course of twenty-two years. She also spent a year writing for American daytime TV dramas *The Guiding Light* and *As the World Turns*, and was offered the position of co-head writer of the former; a million-dollar offer she tearfully turned down. It was scary, turning down an offer that big. But her heart was in her books, and she'd found it impossible to do both.

In March 2014, she did something even scarier. She left the world's largest publisher and went "indie."

Now, she is embarking on an exciting new leg of her publishing journey, with most of her titles moving to small press publisher, Oliver Heber Books.

Maggie writes small town contemporary romances like the recent *Bliss in Big Falls* series, which boasts "a miracle in every story."

She cut her teeth on western themed category romances like her classic 90s and early 2000s *The Texas Brand* and *The Oklahoma All-Girl Brands*, and later expanded into romantic suspense and thrillers like *The Secrets of Shadow Falls* and *The Brown and de Luca Novels*.

She is perhaps best known for her beloved paranormal romances, like the brand new *Fatal series* and perennial favorites *The Immortals*, the *By Magic series*, and *Wings in the Night*.

Maggie is a fifteen-time RITA® Award nominee and one-time winner. She lives in the rolling green and forested hilltops of Cortland County NY, wine & dairy country, despite having sworn off both. She is a vegan Wiccan hippy living her best life with her beloved husband Lance, and usually at least two dogs.

Maggie also writes spiritual self-help and runs an online magic shop, BlissBlog.org

Visit Maggie at www.maggieshayne.com

Ingram Content Group UK Ltd.
Milton Keynes UK
UKHW040644070623
423021UK00004B/85

9 781648 392993